The Original Baby Boomer

By

Bob O'Kelley

DANCING CROWS
PRESS

By Bob O'Kelley
Edited by Dr. Elyse Wheeler PHD
ISBN 13: 978-0-9704420-7-9
ISBN 10: 0-9704420-7-6

ACKNOWLEDGEMENTS
Dr. Ben Kennedy PHD, Claudia Kennedy, Anne
O'Kelley. Fay Kelley, The Carrollton Creative
Writers Club and a special thanks to Dr. Elyse
Wheeler and as always Brenda Hilton

FORWARD

At a military base known as Q-West in Iraq in 2006, I talked with several young soldiers over chow in what I called a chow hall and they called a DFAC (pronounced defac). DFAC is an acronym for dining facility in the modern Army. Why it was necessary to change the name, I have no idea. I worked as a civilian truck driver there from early in 2006 to mid-2011.

I told the young soldiers I worked with about my experiences in Vietnam, and was amazed by how little they knew about my war and my times, the war and times that defined my life. Some did not know we had a draft.

"You mean they made you go into the Army?" one soldier asked. He was surprised, and I was surprised he didn't know. I felt as though my generation's story was being lost. The next day I began this book.

I wrote it with the young in mind, but as it has happened, the old folks relate well to the story. One encouraged her grandson to read it by saying, "If you want to find out how the world we live in got the way it is today, read this book." That was my goal. Not only did I want to capture the events of the period, I wanted to capture the feelings and emotions as well. History can be dull and dry. I pray I have made it come alive.

1

Vietnam 1970

I wasn't as miserable as it sounds. My feet were wrinkled. Dry socks were not to be found anywhere in Echo Company. I hadn't eaten in five days, but that was my fault. Pig that I am; I ate my rations too quickly. I had timed it so my food ran out when our mission ended, or so I thought. I ran out first, but said nothing to Captain Yeager. By now others were out of food as well. No one complained.

All of us lay in shelters made of ponchos tied with boot laces to the foliage. We waited for the monsoon to slow enough for the helicopters to land. Our mission was over. We were to stand down in Duc Pho for a short in country R&R.

McCoy is dead. God, I miss him. It happened the day before the rain started. McCoy, then the Viet Cong girl we killed. An eye for an eye, her death to be our revenge, but the satisfaction hid from us in the jungle, and the jungle mocked us as it always did. It has no mercy. The strong eat the weak. Plants fight for room, sunlight, and the soil's nutrients, yet I saw beauty in the jungle's cruelty.

Is there beauty in war? Perhaps in dying for a just cause there is, maybe in valor. I wondered about my fate, and I wondered why me? *War is ugly. God, it's ugly.*

I sat up with my poncho over my shoulders and my head in its hood, listening to the rain thump on it and stared into the jungle thinking.

War whispers, *"You are alive,"* and war yells, *"You are alive,"* and death comes without fanfare. Your brother is there, then he is gone. Time to grieve, there is none.

Of all the missions, this hurt the most. *They killed McCoy. Goddamnit, McCoy is dead.* We heard a shot, then more. I hit the ground. McCoy did too, but with a bullet hole in his heart. I screamed for the medic. I lay in his blood and returned fire, but it ended as quickly as it started.

I am scarred by the sight of McCoy in a hoist, as they raised him, lifeless, bloody, head drooped, swinging in the air to a helicopter.

It flew away. It flew away, done, gone. That's it. Get on with your day. Hear me! Get on with your day. "Vengeance is mine sayeth the Lord." Fuck that!

I wanted revenge. Jesus or not, I wanted revenge. I felt my mother's me dying away.

"Put a mech on the trail tonight," Captain Yeager said as we made camp.

"Gladly." I led four of us back to the trail we had used. We set a booby-trap. The Army called it a mech, short for mechanized ambush.

Next morning there was a fog making streaks of light between the trees as the sun shone through it. The jungle grew thin where we stopped for the night. The light added another dimension. I felt small. I was a part of it now, the war, the jungle. I was a monkey, a tiger, a leech, or anything else that lived in the jungle. My face had lost its bright shine.

We heard an explosion.

"Sounds like you've caught something in your trap, Rinehart. Saddle up men. Let's go see what it is," Captain Yeager said.

Step by step Echo Company inched to the sound, stopping, listening, then moving. We heard a high-pitched moaning sound that vibrated deep in me. My soul harmonized in sympathy with it. Moans are the same in any language, and they blend well with the other jungle sounds. Jungle is not offended by death. It lives because death begets life. I pushed the bushes away. The torso of a Viet Cong woman lay on the ground. Death crept to her in the jungle's shadows. The mech had blown off her legs. That instant, she became a part of me. She joined McCoy and the others. I carry them all. I carry them all with me, everywhere, every day.

"Goddamnit, a woman," I said.

"What the hell are you talking about? She'd kill you as fast as a man. That bitch wasn't alone. No telling how many of her buddies are out there hiding in the bush just waiting to fire us up."

He sprayed her with M-16 fire. His act was merciful, but I could see in his face he enjoyed it. The man called himself Buck. He was not a friend.

Then the rain started.

2

Five days later, the rain slowed enough for the helicopters to land. We flew to our fire base at San Juan Hill where we bathed and left our gear. Then we made the fifteen-minute flight to our headquarters at Duc Pho for the party.

At Duc Pho, our First Sergeant showed us where we were to sleep. We walked to the mess hall for hot chow, then to the Enlisted Man's Club for beers and the party. That night a band was to play. They came from the Philippines. Filipinos were good imitators of American rock and roll.

We arrived at the club before the show began, so we had sucked down plenty of beer when they began to play. The two girl singers stood aside and danced while a male singer opened the show with a popular song:

> War
> What is it good for?
> Absolutely nothing
> War
> What is it good for?
> Absolutely nothing. . .

We stood with beers in hand and sang along and stamped our feet after the word war. Dust rose from the floor.

I drank, listened, and watched the Filipino girls. It grew dark. I staggered outside, drunk, and leaned against a sandbag structure of some kind, looking up at the night sky. From it McCoy came to me. *"Death is not so bad,"* he said. "It's okay, really. Death is okay."

"McCoy, I love you," I said.

"I know," he said as he faded. Then the Viet Cong girl from the mech came to me.

"Where are my legs?" she said. "Where. . . are. . . my. . . motherfucking legs?"

"I'm sorry. I'm sorry," I cried, and I must have said it aloud. Next I heard a voice from outside me.

"Goddamn, Rick Rinehart, you gotta drink a lot of three-point-two beer to get that drunk."

I looked to see who had spoken to me, "Carter! What in the hell are you doing here?" Carter and I were on the same mortar team in training back at Fort Polk. We spent our leave together partying in Baton Rouge. He was the only man from my training that I called friend.

"As little as possible," he said. He was thinner than the last time I had seen him. There was little that distinguished him from the other soldiers, all dressed alike and all with the same haircut. I never knew him with enough hair to see what color it was.

"Are you in the mortar platoon here?"

"No, let's just say I'm in supply."

"What do you mean by 'let's just say?' Let's just say I'm in America. Either you are or you aren't."

"I am."

"How did you get out of mortars?"

"It's all in who you know, my friend. It's all in who you know."

"Well, just who the hell do you know?"

"Never mind that. Listen, I live in a cool bunker and, get this, I've got a couple of hooch girls over there. Come over and we'll party." He put his hand to his mouth and acted as if he were smoking a joint.

"Girls, where did you get girls?"

"They work on base and they work for me."

"What are you doing, running a house of ill repute over there?"

"Naw, man, I'm running a house of everything repute, and I'm making money hand over fist. I'm gonna re-up when the time comes."

"You're out of your fucking mind. We've got fewer than two months left here, and my ass is going home. You had better believe that."

He and another man lived in a bunker separate from the other soldiers. The bunker was not like any I had seen in Vietnam. It had two rooms, partly underground. The lower part was made of concrete. They made the upper part in the usual army way with wood and sand bags. A stairway led down to the rooms. When he opened the door, I heard music and smelled incense. "Come on baby, light my fire. Come on baby, light my fire." The Doors debut album played. We walked down the stairs and through a beaded door curtain. The beads thumped against the doorjamb as we entered. He had covered

8

the walls in rock and roll posters. In a Vietnamese accent, a pretty girl said, "Light my fire, Carter?" Another pretty Vietnamese girl sat nearby. Both were young and petite. Both wore their black hair long in the Vietnamese style, but wore western jeans and blouses.

"This is Cam and this is Kim," he said, "Cam is my girl."

She kissed him on the cheek. "Carter, you crazy," she said.

I sat by Kim. Carter opened a drawer and pulled out the largest bag of pot I had ever seen and rolled a joint, lit it, took a drag off it, and passed it to Cam.

"How do you get away with this?"

"By keeping the motherfuckers happy; I get'em what they need," he said.

The joint came to Kim. "No, no, I no want," Kim said. She passed it to me. I inhaled the magic vapors.

"Kim is yours. It's on the house," Carter said. He pointed to the other room. I took her hand. We went in, but I was too drunk to perform. We lay together in the nude and talked in broken English as best we could.

"It's okay, baby, you do better when you not drunk," she said.

A woman, a soft woman lay beside me. I had seen only a few women since landing at San Juan Hill more than ten months ago now. They don't live in the remote jungle where I spent my time, and if they did, they were Viet Cong or NVA soldiers.

A woman, a soft nude woman lay beside me. I fell asleep. When I awoke, she still lay with me. She touched me, then sat astride me, and when we finished I said, "Thank you. I needed that." She seemed surprised I thanked her.

"It's okay, baby, I like fuck you. I like you. You good man, Carter bad man. You smell it? You see?"

"What do you mean? Carter is a good guy. What is that smell?"

"You no know? Look." I looked through the door.

Cam lay on the bed asleep or passed out. Carter injected himself with heroin. A military issue heat tab burned on a plate, and a spoon sat beside it on his footlocker.

"Kim, do you do that?"

"No."

"Does Cam?"

"Yes, she's my cousin."

"Get out of here before you get fucked up on that stuff."

"Cannot go at night. Guards stop me. I be okay. You see. I be okay."

I stepped into the room where Carter sat. He looked up with drugged eyes that wanted to close. "Hey, buddy; I got just what you need."

"No, the hell you don't."

"Hey, now, hold on, I'm not fucked up on this stuff."

"The hell you aren't."

I walked to our platoon's assigned barracks. It was full. I found another. No one else was in it. I lay on a bare mattress and in my sleep I saw them all, Jake, Connie, Travis, and Nancy. Then Marianne came. We made love. We made love like we did back at Foster's Store in college while we listened to Crosby, Stills, and Nash.

3

September 2, 1965

Jake and I considered ourselves avant garde, just a little more hip than the others at Atlanta's Therrell High. Connie was pretty cool too, and good looking. Jake was my best friend, and a bit of an oaf, at least I thought so, but what are best friends for if you can't think them a little goofy. Connie was my ex-girlfriend. She wasn't goofy.

On this day, I turned on the portable stereo mom and dad had given me for Christmas. "For college," they said. I didn't believe in Santa Clause, but I did expect him to give me presents. Perhaps that is an oxymoron.

The album I played was also a present. Jake had given it to me for my birthday. The big black record slid down the spindle and the arm raised then lowered the needle into place. Bob Dylan sang, "The Times They are a Changing." The song became the baby boomers' anthem.

"He's the latest thing from Greenwich Village," Jake told me as he handed me the album. I had never heard of Bob Dylan. "Can't sing a lick," is the way most described his sound, rough, thick, and nasal and his guitar playing basic, but his music struck deep in me. I did not know why.

My father didn't cuss, at least not around the family. He had grown used to the sounds of rock and roll vibrating through my bedroom door, but this was different. He opened the door, stuck his head in, then said, "What in the goddamn hell are you listening to." He was a Frank Sinatra man. I switched to an album that was not as offensive to his ears. I played the Beatles *I Wanna Hold Your Hand*, over and over. I danced in front of the mirror until the phone rang.

"Hello."

"Hey." It was Jake.

"What do you want, ass-breath?"

"What are you wearing? My dad says I should wear a coat and tie. I told him we were going to college, not a funeral. What are you going to do?"

"My dad said the same thing, and Jake."

"What?"

"It is always better to over dress than underdress." My father was in the tuxedo business and that was practically the family motto.

"Okay, see you there."

Jake, Connie, and I were to be freshmen at West Georgia College. Today we were going to orientation.

I went back to my dancing and dressing. By now the Beatles sang, "She was just seventeen, Do you know what I mean?" I did know what they meant.

The phone rang again. This time mom answered it then called to me, "Rick, it's Connie."

"Hello," I said.

"My dad wants to know if he can follow you guys. He's never been to the campus."

"You know Campbelton Road, don't you?"

"Of course."

"That's route 166. Just follow it for fifty miles. The school is on it after you go through Carrollton, can't miss it."

"Okay, see you there."

Connie lived close by. From the time we were babies, the world had pushed us together, in the beginning because it was cute and as teenagers because it was safe and convenient. At sixteen she was my girlfriend, but by title only. I never did more than kiss her good night at the door. The charade lasted until we both began to want to see other people. It ended with the classic words, "I love you but not in that way," and I did love Connie and I wasn't sure in what way. She was a pixie cut blond, good looking and fun.

My mind tends to wander when I ride. On the way to orientation that day, it did. I wandered if Connie and Jake were ahead of us or behind, then I wandered what Connie looked like with no clothes on, then I wandered why I was denied my proper rank and status in the world's pecking order. I am the original baby boomer, the first of my kind, heir to the throne. I came to that conclusion when I was sixteen. World War II ended in August of 1945 with the surrender of Japan. In May of that year, the Germans surrendered in Europe where my father served. He was on a ship on the way to fight the Japanese when Truman dropped the bomb and ended it. His ship was near Boston. It docked there. Dad's whole unit was discharged. A day later he was home in Atlanta, long before anyone else. He and mom drove to Vogel State Park in the mountains north of Atlanta, and there I was conceived. Nine months less one day later, I was born. I am the first baby that was conceived by a returning soldier from World War II. I am . . . the original . . . baby boomer. Hold your applause.

I told my dad when I discovered this.

"So what?" he said.

"Don't you think that makes me special?"

"No."

So I told my mom.

"That's nice, son."

"Mom, don't you think that makes me special?"

"You are always special to me, son."

4

I tried to convince myself that I was not nervous as we neared the college. I failed. My stomach knotted as we turned onto Front Campus Drive, but I acted as nonchalant as possible, not wanting my father to see me sweat. Though he never spoke of it, he had been man enough to face the Nazis in the war. *Confronting a college is nothing compared with confronting a Nazi,* I thought. *I don't know. Maybe it is a different kind of fear.*

We parked. The unair-conditioned gym where the orientation was to take place was hot and humid. Wooden folding chairs had been set up on the basketball court. They creaked as students and parents squirmed, trying to get comfortable. Suit coats came off, and perspiration adhered to the ladies' faces, except the pretty girls. Why is it that pretty girls never perspire? Perhaps, it is because they have it made. Who knows? As for me, my shirt clung to my back, glued there by moisture. I didn't have it made. I was sure of that.

I found Jake and Connie without a problem. Jake's shirttail hung out and his hair hung wet in his face, but Connie sat fresh and crisp as though the temperature was sixty degrees. Like I said, pretty girls . . . I gave Connie a hug, and punched Jake in the shoulder. He flipped me off underhanded so that the adults would not see.

Dr. Boyd, the college president made a rah rah speech about how well we were going to do in life, then lectured us on the rules. He took questions from the parents. Then it was over. Time to move our stuff into the dorm. Time to kiss mom good-bye and shake dad's hand. Time to stumble away from the nest.

Jake and I were to be roommates in Strozier Hall, the newest building on campus. It didn't take us long to get our things moved in. I had a foot locker, a record player, a portable typewriter and a few clothes. That was it. Jake had the same.

"Don't let the door knob hit you in the ass," Jake said when the door clicked shut as our parents left us, alone, on our own, for the first time.

"Free, at last," I said.

"Now, what?" He said.

"We're free."

"Yeah, so?"

"What do we do."

"I don't know."

"Drink beer?"

"We don't have any."

"Try this, then" He said as he pulled the latest edition of Playboy from his trunk.

"Oh, yeah, look at her," I said as I flipped to the centerfold.

"I'll bet Hugh Hefner gets laid more than any man in America." Hefner was the publisher of *Playboy*. I held the centerfold so that Jake could see.

"I'd slide down a five-foot razor blade and sit in a bucket of lemon juice if I could do it with her," he said.

"I'd slide down the same razor blade and sit in a bucket of lemon juice if I could do it with anybody, just once.

"You're too damn goofy."

"It takes one to know one." I said.

Jake and I were too cool to admit our virginity to others, but I couldn't fool him and he couldn't fool me. We knew each other too well.

"No, on second thought, I wouldn't slide down a razor blade and sit in a bucket of lemon juice just to get to do it. It would hurt too much," I said.

"Yeah, you'd whack your whacker off on the blade. Then where would you be?"

"Singing soprano," I said in a high-pitched voice.

Jake laughed. Old jokes are old to the old, but new to the young.

Dad and I never had the birds and the bees talk. He thought I was smart enough to figure it out by myself, and I did, and I did it without the help of the internet. Mom contributed to my sex education by leaving "Sex for Dummies" lying around where she knew I would find it, but it didn't have pictures. Even *Playboy* didn't show full frontal nudity in those days. It was illegal. I wondered about girls a lot.

"Were in college. Don't you think we should do something besides sit in our room," I said.

"Like what?"

"Go walk around. Be social."

"You're right," Jake said, but neither of us moved.

"We should make our beds, first," Jake said.

"Yeah, we should make our beds and unpack our trunks."

"Yeah, unpack our trunks." Which we did until there was a knock on our door.

I opened it. A young man stood there with his hand out to be shaken, so I shook it for a long time. He said he was Travis Wellman. I introduced myself, then Jake. The conversation died there. *What to talk about? The weather?* Dad had taught me that when you don't know what to say, talk about the weather.

"How's the weather?" I asked.

"What?"

"The weather, how is it?"

Travis looked confused. "Hot," he said.

Jake looked confused too, "Why did you ask that?"

"Just checking."

Jake saved me by asking, "Where are you from, Travis?"

"Cartersville."

"Where is that?" Jake asked.

"Fifty miles north of Atlanta, kinda in the mountains."

"You're a country boy," I teased.

"And proud of it," he said.

Travis was a tall dirty-blond with square shoulders and a good shape. He was good looking. At least, the girls thought so. I couldn't see it myself. He had a way with women and several notches on his gun handle which was more than Jake and I could say.

"Seen the new *Playboy*?" Jake asked fearing the conversation might reach another lull and I would talk about the weather again.

"Naw."

He threw it to Travis who studied the centerfold then said, "Wouldn't it be great if the girls could go topless on campus?"

"They wouldn't do it," Jake said.

"Are you kidding me? It's against the rules for them to be on campus in shorts. They wear long rain coats when they walk to gym class so you can forget topless," I said.

"I know. I know. I was kidding."

"I'm hungry," Jake said, then looked at Travis. Jake was always hungry.

"Me, too," Travis said. He was always hungry as well. Come to think about it, so was I.

"Don't I remember something about having to wear a coat and tie to the cafeteria on Sundays?" I said.

"Yeah, I remember reading something about that," Travis said.

"I'll look it up." I flipped through the handbook. "No, that's at lunch. I guess they want you to look as if you had gone to church whether you did or not."

Travis walked to the door, opened it, and then said. "My cousin told me that when he went to school here a few years ago, if you were on campus over the weekend, going to church was required."

"In a state school?" I asked.

"Yep."

"How could they tell that you didn't go?" Jake asked.

"Maybe they called roll in the church," Travis said.

I continued reading the dress code. They stopped and listened.

"Men are to wear slacks, no jeans, and shirts with collars. Women must wear dresses or skirts and blouses. Pants or jeans are not allowed."

"That's a good thing," Jake said.

"Why's that?" Travis asked as he walked out the door.

Jake followed behind him. "So we can look up their skirts." He said.

I couldn't resist taunting Jake. "That's the only way you will ever see a snatch."

"You got no room to talk," Jake said, looking wounded.

"Sorry, Jake, I shouldn't have said that."

"Fuck you," he said, and we began our walk. Who knows where the cafeteria is?" I asked.

Jake walked behind me, "Under the gym where we had orientation," he said.

Travis was behind Jake. "That's a long walk from here," he said.

Connie and several acquaintances from her dorm joined us in our walk. She surprised me with a passionate hug. Travis noticed. "Is this your girlfriend?"

"No. I am not his girlfriend. I used to be, but we broke up. We're still friends, though."

"Nobody stays friends after they break up," Travis said.

"We did." To prove it she kissed my cheek. "See, I still like him."

"Woo, woo," I said while I reached out with my hands as if I were going to fondle her breast. She slapped me.

"See there. She hit me but I'm not mad," I said.

"Pig," Connie said, but she walked close to me. We found the cafeteria under the gym as Jake had predicted, and got in the line which ran outside.

"I don't know whether that food tastes as good as it smells, but it sure smells good. I hope it's better than high school. We gotta eat it three times a day."

The day was warm, so the cafeteria's wooden doors were open. To keep insects out, there were screen doors, and as each person entered it banged when the spring slammed it shut. The granite step at the door's base had a dip worn into it from shoe after shoe stepping on it year after year. Inside, a gray-headed lady punched our meal tickets with a handheld punch, and we were ready for our first West Georgia meal, fried chicken, rice and gravy, green beans, creamed corn, your choice of rolls or cornbread, and sweet or unsweet tea. We are in the South, after all.

Births, deaths, marriages, and graduations are life-changing events, but often the inconsequential things are also life-changing. They go unnoticed. My father did not know that sitting beside my mother on a streetcar in 1939 would lead to a marriage, me, and my brothers. On this day, God dealt a new card in the life game, though I didn't understand that then.

When I saw her, I said, "Who's that?"

Connie turned around, "Who?"

"That girl over there." I held my tray, so I pointed with my elbow.

"How do I know? Remember, I just got here, too."

I stared. Connie noticed.

"Good grief, put your tongue back in your mouth."

"She looks like Snow White."

"Who? Her?"

"You know, Snow White and the seven dwarfs."

"Yeah, I can kinda see that what with her black hair and all. She is gorgeous. You ought to see your face. I'm jealous."

"Why? You won't give me the time of day."

After dinner, we returned to Strozier Hall. We went to bed at midnight, and my first day of college ended.

5

At exactly the time I started college, Berry McGuire recorded "The Eve of Destruction." One line in it said, "You're old enough to kill but not for voting." I thought about that a lot.

Most would say I'm sociable, and I am, but I can get enough. By the end of the first week, I had had enough of the shaving cream fights, socks stuffed in sleeping mouths, seeing how far you could slide in your socks on the highly waxed hall floor, and all the other hoopla that goes on in a freshman dorm. I needed a break, so I walked to the student center, put some nickels in the jukebox and listened to Otis Redding while reading a newspaper I found left lying around.

The headline read, "President Johnson Sends More Troops to Vietnam." Soon there would be two-hundred-thousand there, then half a million, but we did not know that then.

Just before I finished high school, two friends showed up one day at school in National Guard uniforms, and I thought they were cool. I knew girls liked men in military uniforms. That would soon change.

At dinner that night, I said, "Dad, I think I am going to join the National Guard." He continued eating his soup with a slurp at each spoonful and did not acknowledge my statement. By his silence, I knew I was not going to join the National Guard.

I soon grew tired of the student center. People kept playing the same boring song. I heard "Hush, Hush Sweet Charlotte" all I cared to hear it. I was running out of nickels to fight back, so I walked outside and sat under a big oak on the soft grass. The five o'clock sun was soothing, and I soon fell asleep, only to be awakened by someone saying, "Wake up, Rick, before you sleep through dinner.

"Oh, hey, Charles," I said. Charles was a friend from high school. I knew he was enrolled at West Georgia, but this was the first time I had seen him on campus. He was a sophomore. "Wanna sit with me? We've got a little time." Charles joined me under the tree.

"I'm leaving school," he said.

"Why?"

"I'm going in the National Guard."

"Why?"

"So I don't have to go to Vietnam. I'm close to flunking out. I will lose my student draft deferment, and you know what that means.

"Yeah, you'll get drafted."

"In the Guard, all I do is go to basic training for six months, and then go to a meeting once a month and to camp for two weeks each summer until I get out. That's it. They can't draft you when you are already in the military. Everyone in America knows they are not going to use the Guard in this war. You ought to think about joining before it's too late. The Guard units are filling fast."

"I already tried. My old man won't have it. He says that little war will be over long before I graduate and they will quit drafting. Probably there will be too many people in the Army by then and they will need to get rid of some troops. I never heard of Vietnam until a few weeks ago. Had you?"

"No, I'm against communism, but I don't want to get killed halfway around the world fighting for a country I never heard of."

6

By the end of my first quarter, I was in trouble. All my grades were good except English 101. I made a B in Math 110, an A in Sociology, an A in PE, but . . . in English I did not make a C, I did not make a D, I made a flat F. It made my father unhappy and it made me even more unhappy. The problem started on the first day of class.

"Write about what you did last summer." Mr. Carpenter said.

I fidgeted in my desk. *Ahum, a, oooh, a, hum. What did I do last summer? Oh, yeah, I worked at my Dad's store. So what! That's not interesting. This is college. It must be profound. What profound thing did I do last summer? Nothing! I haven't done anything profound in my life. I know. I'll lie. I went on a skiing trip to Colorado. No, no, you don't ski in the summer, dumb-ass. I did go to Panama City. Big deal, everybody in Georgia does that. I know. I climbed Mount Kilimanjaro like Hemingway. He's profound. Naw, Carpenter will never buy it.*

The clock ticked. Time began to run out. *I gotta write something.* In the last few minutes, I did. It wasn't profound. It also wasn't punctuated right or spelled right. When he returned our graded papers, he called me to his desk.

"Mr. Rinehart, what did you mean by this?" he said as he gave my paper to me. Across its front, he wrote a big F. I unfolded the paper and began to read it. It made no sense. I wrote it; still, it made no sense, even to me.

"Mr. Carpenter," I said, "when I wrote this only God and I knew what it meant. Now, God only knows." I took my seat. Things went downhill from there.

He wanted the next theme to be written out of class and typed. From my closet, I pulled out my graduation present, a Royal portable typewriter. I took typing in high school. Few males did then. The world of typing belonged to the female.

I felt as if I were Hemingway. He used a manual typewriter with a two-finger hunt-and-peck method, but I could type right. I wondered did that make me a better writer than him. He was my hero.

Tap, tap, tap, tap, oops. I pulled the page out and started over. Tap, tap, tap, tap, tap, tap, tap, tap, tap, tap, tap, tap, tap, tap, tap, tap, oops, I pulled the page out and started over again.

The year was 1965. White-out didn't exist until 1966. Tap, tap, tap, tap, tap, tap, tap, oops, after eight hours, I wrote a two-page theme. This time I made it profound, but it still contained misspelled words, punctuation errors, and, now, typos to boot. I got an F. *I'll do better on the next theme,* and I did. I got a D. By the fifth week, there was no doubt, I would fail. I stopped going to class, but I did show up for the final.

"Write a theme about how you felt on your first day on campus," Mr. Carpenter said. I sat at my desk and fidgeted again. *Ahum, a, oooh, a, hum, oh, the hell with it.* I wrote I felt like shit, signed my name, and walked out. A few days later, someone from my English class cornered me in the cafeteria. "Mr. Carpenter said to give this to you." He had written a big red C on it with the note, "A great improvement over your previous work. Needs to be longer."

I took English 101 again the next quarter but made a D. All my other grades were good, but my

English grades put me at risk of flunking out, so I waited a few quarters to build up my grade point average before trying it again. The instructor called me aside. She said, "I understand this course has given you problems. Here is how you can pass it. Write simple sentences that you can punctuate correctly. Quit trying to use words you cannot spell. Keep it simple. Never, ever try to be profound. You can't make an A this way, but you can make a C." I did as she said and got a C on every paper I turned in.

I think all humankind should drop to its collective knees, and thank God and Bill Gates for Microsoft Word. Never take it for granted. Love it. Microsoft Word makes you smarter than you are. If I were writing this book on a Royal, portable typewriter without white-out, there would be no book, and maybe no me, for I would have surely died of nervous frustration. God bless Papa Hemingway and all the others who used typewriters.

Connie and I ate lunch at twelve –thirty. We always sat together. The arrangement suited us. Upper classmen with cars began asking her out. I wanted to date too, but freshmen were not allowed cars, which effectively meant they couldn't date. The freshmen boys were a lonely lot.

At lunch she asked, "What did you do last night?"   "Nothing special, I studied and bullshitted with the guys. What'd you do?"

"I had a date!"

"Oh, yeah. Who did you go out with?"

"You don't know him."

"Does he have a name?"

"Danny James. He's a junior."

"Danny James. You're right. I don't know him. What'd you do?"

"Went to the movies."

"What did you see?"

"*What's New Pussycat?*"

The next day, we talked again. When she asked what I did the night before, I answered the same way. "Nothing special, I studied and bullshitted with the guys. What'd you do?"

"I had a date."

"Again!"

Bill Martin was his name this time. She saw *What's New Pussy Cat?* again. Next day, she dated Ben Brown and saw *What's New Pussycat?* for a third time. I'll admit I became jealous, and I think she could see it.

"You ought to ask Snow White out," Connie said.

"Who?"

"Snow White. You know. You named her that. The girl in the cafeteria line you saw on our first night here. Just call her up and ask her for a date."

"You make it sound so easy. Do you know how hard it is to call somebody you don't really know and ask them out? Besides, I don't know her name."

"Well, find out, and figure out a way to meet her. Flirt. Do I have to teach you everything?"

7

I had the wrong idea about college. At least, I had the wrong idea about a small college in a small Georgia town in 1965. I expected Greenwich Village. I got Mayberry, but that's okay. I have a multifaceted personality, and Barney Fife is one.

Today, Carrollton, Georgia is what I wanted it to be in 1965. It has a quaint square with chic boutiques, good restaurants, college bars, bookstores, and coffee shops. The new cultural arts center sits right off the square. The University of West Georgia hosts cultural events as well. Local talent is in abundance, artists, potters, country bands, rock groups and such.   .

I came to Carrollton half a century too early. In 1965, there were no bars or coffee shops, only one movie theater, and just a few restaurants. Carrollton had nothing for the students to do, and to exacerbate the problem, the college did not allow fraternities. That's why the county fair was such a big deal to us.

Travis made friends with Bill, an upperclassman with a car, and because of this "good buddiness," he had transportation and many dates. He did well with the girls. Jake and I envied him.

He came into our room one night. "You guys want to go to the fair? We can ride with Bill."

"Sure," Jake and I said.

The night of the fair we stopped at the Bay Station to buy beer. Everyone at West Georgia knew students could buy beer there, no questions asked. We each bought a six-pack.

"Now what?" I said.

Bill sat in the driver's seat but did not crank the engine. "I don't know."

Jake looked up, "Me neither."

Travis who sat in the front seat turned to face Jake and me in the back. "I know. Out by the airport there is a deserted road. Let's go there." Bill headed to the airport. He parked in a secluded spot.

Click Ka-Pop Kc-Ssshhh, sounded four times as each opened his beer can. The sun still hung in the sky. We looked at each other. We sipped our beer. We sat. We sipped. We looked at each other. We sat. We sipped. We sat. We looked at each other. We had nothing to talk about. Everything had already been said in the long nights of conversation back at the dorm. We sat. We sipped. Finally, Jake said, "I don't think sitting in a car on a dirt road drinking beer is much fun. It's boring as hell, and we got all this beer to drink."

"Well, drink up, and let's get out of here," Travis said. We sucked down our beers as fast as we could without puking. It became a race. Travis won. We peed then headed to the fair.

When we got there, Jake said, "I gotta pee again." We all did. Porta-potties sat in a row next to the parking lot. We made a beeline in their direction; only my beeline was more like a bee S. *Jesus, I'm drunk. . . . I wanted to get a little high, but not like this.*

I made it to the porta-potty all right, but a long line of people waited to use it. *I gotta pee. I gotta pee. I gotta pee, hurry, hurry, hurry.* I made it, *Thank God.* I peed. Jake and Bill threw up in the porta-potties they used. Travis and I did not.

As we walked I wondered if anyone could tell how drunk I was. *I know. I'll smile a lot. Then they won't know.* We walked from the porta-potties to the fairground. The carnival sounds came to us. Screams from the distant carnival rides were heard first. Rock and roll from the Rock'n Rotor Antigravity Machine came next, then Calliope music from the merry-go-round, then rumbles and screeches from the Wild Mouse. It blended into a carnival harmony.

Next, the smells came. Each entered our nostrils with their characteristic charisma. The aromas from cotton candy, peanuts, popcorn, funnel cakes, and foot-long hotdogs covered in sweet-smelling onions brought memories of past fairs.

And then came the sights. They churned into one confusing, brightly-colored blur for me and made me dizzy. I looked away from anything that swirled. A clown taunted me as I walked, by rubbing one index finger over the other in a sign of shame. *The fair isn't fun when you're too drunk to ride anything,* I thought. *Yeah, but I'm cool.*

A man who stood in front of a tent called to us, "Hey, hey, come here a minute."

Travis turned, "Who, me?"

"Yeah, you," the man said. We walked over to him. He leaned forward as if he were going to tell us something confidential. "You boys want to see some pussy?"

Travis looked directly at the man, "What do you mean?" The man pointed to a sign, "Hoochee Coochee Show, fifty cents," it said.

"Fifty cents! That's a lot. We could ride the Wild Mouse for that," Travis said.

"Yeah, but it's worth it," he said in a low voice dripping with artificial sincerity.

Jake's eyes filled with lust. "Do they get naked?"

"Naked as the day they were born," the man answered.

"Oh, bullshit, mister, that's against the law," I said.

"This is the county fair. The law is different for us. It's not against the law here."

"Are they good-looking?" Jake asked.

"Yep, they're about your age." I wanted to go in, but I didn't want to be too anxious in front of Travis and Bill, least they discover my ignorance of the opposite sex. I knew Jake wanted to go in, too. He knew nothing about the female anatomy other than what *Playboy* had shown him. "Let's do it," I said. All agreed.

Inside, a stage stood surrounded by twenty-five men of all types, young and old, rich and poor.

Silence made the air tense. No one spoke, and there was no music. The only lights were the spot lights focused on the stage. The curtain was made from tent canvas, and through it, without announcement or fanfare, two nude, attractive young girls stepped in for the men to study. The girls said nothing. They stood. The men looked. Finally, one said, "How y'all doing?" and the icy atmosphere disappeared.

"Fine," the men responded.

"Better, now that you're here, baby," someone in a red cap and overalls yelled.

They pranced back and forth on the stage taking caps and glasses from those who stood close, and rubbed them in their pubic area. "Here's a little souvenir for you, honey," they said as they gave the objects back. They continued their walk, making sure all got a good look.

"Where y'all from?" someone yelled.

"Talladega, Alabama."

"How'd you get this job?"

"When this fair came to our town, we asked for it, just like you get any other job."

One began doing something with Ping-Pong balls and a cigarette that I had no idea was possible.

"What are your names?"

"I'm Nan. She's Lucy."

"How old were you the first time you did it?"

"Fourteen," Nan answered. They bent over with their backsides to the audience. Nan turned and squatted with her legs apart. "I don't know why y'all wanna see this." She stood. "It ain't nothing you ain't never seen before 'cept maybe you young ones over there." She pointed directly at me.

"Have, too. And I'll bet I'm as old as you are."

"You look a little wet behind the ears to me. You're kinda cute, though. I'll tell you what. Meet me after the last show, and I'll get you caught up on things," she said as she left the stage.

As we walked out, the man in the red cap and overalls slapped me on the back, "Boy, you got it made," he said. "If I was you, I'd take her up on that." He slapped my back again. He leaned over me with his arm still on my back, looked directly into my face, and said, "You got it made, ain't ya, boy, huh, huh." He slapped my back again. "Yeah, yeah, got it made. I'm tellin ya buddy. Got it made." He walked away, and I felt as if I were crawling from a sewer.

Outside, the Satellite Ride spun. Its rotating lights made me dizzy again. I staggered. The semisweet smell of funnel cakes cooking nearby filled the air, nauseating me. I wanted to go back to the car and lie down.

"Rick, Rick." *Someone is calling me.* I turned to see who called. "Connie. My sweet Connie, is it really you?"

"I've got someone I want you to meet. Oh, shit, you're drunk as a skunk." I staggered. My eyes focused. Snow White stood beside Connie. . . .

8

The next day was Friday. I was too hungover to go to class. Connie went home for the weekend, so I did not see her until Monday at lunch. I sat in our usual place. She walked to me with her tray, dropped it on the table so hard she almost toppled her tea, then slid into the chair just as my Mother did when she was angry. "Did you have fun at the fair?"

"Not really."

"Well, you should have as drunk as you were."

"Hey, you don't have a lot of room to talk. Remember that night we went to see Mike at the Kappa Sig House at Tech?"

"Yeah, well, at least you didn't have to carry me to the car. You're lucky you didn't get arrested."

"Who carried me to the car?"

"Jake and Travis."

"I don't remember that. They didn't say anything about it."

"Do you remember Marianne?"

"Who's Marianne?"

"Marianne Morgan, Snow White, you don't remember; do you?"

"Oh, no, did I meet her?"

"No, you puked all over her before I could introduce you. I mean, you got her good, from her hair to her shoes, and on her face, too. We had to go back to the dorm."

"Oh, no . . . You're lying. Tell me you're lying."

"No, the hell I'm not."

"What do I do now?"

"Apologizing would be a good start, but I don't think it will do any good. You might as well get infatuated with someone else. You've blown it, buddy. We saw you coming out of that Hoochee Coochee show. She thinks you are a disgusting pig."

I felt like a disgusting pig. I must apologize. I had blown it, but she stayed on my mind. People always want what they can't have. I thought of her even more now. At least I knew her name, Marianne like Marianne on *Gilligan's Island*. Perhaps she was just as sweet.

I began to notice her on campus, watching her from a distance for several days, studying her until I knew her schedule. I stalked her, but it was a genteel stalk, and she did not notice.

She had a boyfriend, a blond upperclassman who drove a red MG. I didn't like him, or his pretentious little English sports car, or his London Fog coat, or his neatly laundered Gant shirts, or his Weejun penny-loafers, or his neatly pressed khaki slacks. Worst of all, I hated the high school letter sweater with the big N on it for Atlanta's Northside High where he ran track. He was a rich Northsider. I grew up in the less affluent Southside, and animosity existed between the two groups.

He walked her to class, except her ten o'clock class. I could talk to her then, where the sidewalk runs under the oaks near the gym. When I saw her coming, I took a friendly stance. She walked toward me with her books cradled to her chest, and was close before she noticed me, and when she did, she stopped. "You aren't going to puke on me again are you?"

"I am so sorry. I was so drunk. I don't remember doing it. Connie told me about it. Please accept my apology."

"Well. . . okay," she said and walked away. I hoped the apology would make me feel better about myself, but it didn't.

Autumn became winter. Outside the cold came, but inside it was cozy, especially in the old buildings that still had steam heat. The radiators sometimes hissed and clanged as though someone with a hammer was hitting them, but their heat warmed your body and your soul. The cafeteria had steam heat too, and the cooking smells from the kitchen made it feel like home.

Connie and I continued our regular lunch date.

She told me about her dates, and I told her about watching a spider crawl across the ceiling while I lay in bed with nothing to do but watch it, or bullshit with the guys or worse yet, study.

"Well, Miss Popularity, what did you do last night," I asked.

"I had a date."

"Imagine that, with who, or should I say with whom?"

"Phil Nixon, he's a senior."

"Oooooh, a senior, coming up in the world, aren't we."

"Oh, shut up. I like him. I like him better than anybody I have dated."

"Better than me? You dated me, remember."

"That was different. I like you, but differently."

"How do you like me?"

"I don't know. Like a bro. . . . Well, not exactly like a brother. Well, you know."

"Yeah, I know."

For the next week, our lunch conversations consisted of one subject, Phil. Phil did this and Phil did that. I asked her, "Are you in love with this Phil guy?"

"I don't know, maybe."

I'll admit I was jealous, but more than that; I was concerned like a big brother. I began to ask others about Phil. None of my friends knew him except Travis. When I asked him about Phil, he said in his country way, "He's the biggest whoredog on campus, gets more pussy than James Bond. I saw him with Connie the other day. She hugged all over him. If he hasn't already nailed her, he's moving in for the kill. I'll guarantee you that, but monogamy ain't exactly his strong suit. He's screwing Becky and some girl named Whitney. If she wants to be his girl, she had better get in line."

"Whoredog!" I had never heard the term, but I understood the meaning. "More pussy than Bond," I must warn Connie before she does something she will regret.

Next day at lunch, I told Connie as tactfully as I could what I learned. Not knowing how she would react, I waited until we finished eating before telling her. I had known Connie so long that I do not remember when I didn't know her. Even so, her response surprised me. Her face turned red. She looked directly into my eyes and said, "You're lying."

"Connie, honey, listen, I know I'm not lying, and I am sure I'm not wrong about this."

"You're lying because you're jealous, and you're jealous because you are in love with me. You have always been in love with me, and I love you too, but not that way."

"Connie, listen. There is some truth in what you say, but it isn't jealousy talking. The big brother side of my feelings for you is doing the talking now. Get out while you can. He will hurt you."

She took her tray and walked away. Next day at lunch, she ignored me.

9

I missed her. Connie had always been in my life. She was my playmate as a child, and she was the first girl I had kissed. Like Jake, she was always there. She was there when I was eight and hated little girls. She was there when I was sixteen and wanted to touch her. Like Mom and Dad, my brother, my house, my bike and my dog Fred, Connie was always there. Now she wasn't.

I sat on a wall near the student center. A group of guys gathered for conversation between classes. A few sat with an open book studying. I sat doing nothing. Connie walked by, said "hey" as if she hardly knew me and went on. As she walked by the guys, their chatter stopped. This did not surprise Connie. She had grown used to stares, and men bumping into solid objects while gawking at her.

After she walked out of earshot, one of the guys said, "That girl is so fine. Phil's fucking her. He said she's hotter than a two-dollar pistol. She went on the pill for him."

"No, shit, I wouldn't mind tapping that, myself," another guy said.

"Fat chance your ugly ass will ever get a girl that fine," the first guy said.

I jumped up with balled fists and walked to the two.

"What's your problem," one said. He took a defensive stance.

"Nothing," I said and sat down. *Why take it out on them? That's killing the messenger.* The two watched me for a minute or so, then returned to their group. "That freshman over there is fucking nuts," I heard one say.

I sat on the wall again, thinking. *Why, why, why would she do it with that asshole and not with me? He is using her. He is using her. Now, she is tarnished.* I walked back to the dorm.

Jake always had the new issue of *Playboy* lying around. He was not alone. More copies of it were on campus than the Bible; far more when you consider some guys had a stack of back issues two feet high. Even the girls read it. They compared themselves with the topless girls in the magazine, and generally found themselves lacking. The airbrushed beauties in the magazine looked more like store mannequins than real women, but I didn't know that then.

Hugh Hefner, *Playboy's* publisher, was a leader in the sexual revolution; even so, his version of it was misogynistic. Women were not equal partners to men, but objects to be exploited as Phil exploited Connie. I didn't think about that then. I had read Hefner's article in the "Playboy Adviser" on "the pill."

He's right, I thought as I lay the magazine aside. *The pill has changed everything, and I am right in the middle of that change. In the past, fear of unwanted pregnancy controlled sex lives, especially for women. Now there would be no fear of pregnancy, freeing women. Connie's world differs from her mother's. The idea that a girl should be a virgin when she married is vanishing, and I am here as it vanishes. Oddly, knowing this made me feel better.*

Two weeks later, I sat alone in the cafeteria with my back to the serving line. Without warning, Connie slipped into the seat in front of me. She did not bring a tray of food; instead, she carried a cup of coffee and a cigarette. Yes, in those days, you could smoke in the cafeteria.

"You were right," she said, then took a puff of her cigarette. I could tell she was an inexperienced smoker by the shallow way she drew the smoke into her lungs.

"When did you start smoking?"

"Never mind that. You were right." I didn't say I told you so.

She continued, "I was mean to you. I'm sorry."

"It's okay, Connie. It's okay."

"No, it's not okay. I loved him, Rick. I loved him, and I fucked him, and he walked away. We talked about marriage. I went on the pill for the bastard, then he just moved on like I was nothing. I fantasize about cutting his fuckin balls off. He deserves it. Bastard. He took my virginity for the goddamn fun of it."

In that one sentence, Connie used more profanity than she had used in her life. *Funny,* I thought, *the "Playboy Adviser" never mentions problems like this. It never mentions anything about the girl's feelings at all.*

All I could think to say was, "It will be okay," but I knew   it was shallow.

"No, the hell it's not okay. I was saving myself for marriage like you are supposed to do."

"Connie, it's 1965. Most men don't expect that anymore."

"I know, I know, but still I wanted to save it for the right one."

"Look at it this way. At the time you did it, he was the right one. Did you like it?"

"Yes, but he's still a bastard."

"Do you want me to knock him into next week for you?"

"Of course not, we're in college, not high school. Besides, you aren't much of a fighter." I knew how she would answer the question before I asked it.

"You're right," I said. "I don't like to fight. I think of myself as more of a lover than a fighter." She laughed.

"Well," she said.

"If you were a guy, losing your virginity would be something to brag about. You want to take mine? Nobody else is interested and you're an experienced woman now."

"I don't think so. You're gonna have to figure that one out on your own."

After that, Connie and I did not continue our lunch date. We knew it was time to go our separate ways, but she will always be my first love, and I hers, and that's special.

10

"In the spring, a young man's fancy turns to thoughts of love," according to Alfred Tennyson's 1842 poem "Locksley Hall," and it was as true in 1965 as it was in 1842. Spring came late that year, but on the first good day of it, students' eyes turned from professors' lectures to the windows, and there was a shuffling of feet, and fidgeting and daydreams, as nature's renewing energy touched us. In 1965, most did not have enough money for a wild time on Spring break in Fort Lauderdale as students do today. Student loans were not common then, and Georgia's HOPE scholarship did not exist. Something else would have to suffice for fun.

On Jones Mill Road in the little town of Whitesburg, there was an old truss-type, one-lane, steel bridge, so old that it may have been built in the late nineteenth century. It had rusted reddish-brown. The builder floored it with wooden beams and planks laid across the beans end to end in the direction of travel. Under it was Snake creek, which ran six feet deep in places after a good rain. Today, water conservation projects have rendered it to a mere trickle, but on this day in 1965, it ran full from spring rains, and near the bridge nature had made a sandy beach.

Good times need little coordination. They just happen, and on this day with little or no forethought, several groups of students descended on the little beach like song birds returning from their winter migration, and with them they brought buckets of fried chicken and plenty of beer. Jake, Travis, and I were among them. I knew some people there, and some I did not.

As if we were at South Beach in Miami, the girls spread their beach towels, drenched themselves in Coppertone and lay in the sun while the guys splashed in the creek. But having splashed in creeks before, and as I loved Coppertone's smell, and as spring had come, and as girls clad in two piece bathing suits sat on the beach, I and several other lascivious young men greased ourselves and lay in the sun with them. Jake, always a big kid at heart, and Travis who needed no more feminine attention, headed for the water. Soon they were diving off the bridge, which stood eight or ten feet above the creek while I talked with the girls.

I made friends with Jamie. We talked of our mutual interest in literature. She was interested literature. I was interested in her, but for a guy who did not pass English 101, I was doing well with my pretending I knew what I was talking about.

"It's so nice to talk to a guy with a brain," she said. She too had a nice brain, but it was her body that drew my attention. Every time she moved it bounced in the right places, and it curved in the right places, but in contrast to her body, her slightly freckled pixie face gave the impression that she was not quite mature. Her hair was auburn and curly, almost in ringlets. I liked the way she looked, and oh, yeah, I liked her brain, too.

She and her friends brought a bottle of vodka that they mixed with grapefruit juice. I drank my beer, and in a little time, we were all loose-mouthed, buzzed, and "everybody is my friend" drunk. With so many girls around me, the air must have been filled with pheromones which stimulated my subconscious. That and the beer and the sun in my eyes, took me to a different world. I squinted. Jamie sat there with the sun directly behind her. She sat close, so close that even I could tell she wanted me to kiss her, so I did, and I did it well. The kiss was long. She responded with a sigh. I wanted to touch her, and she wanted to be touched. We knew. "Let's go for a walk. We'll wade down the creek," I said.

In a soft, long southern drawl, she said, "Okaay."

When I stood, the creek, the sky, all of it spun. I didn't realize how drunk I had gotten. I held my hand out for her to take. She took it and pulled up. "Oh, shit," she said and I knew her world spun, too, maybe more than mine.

As we walked away arm in arm, one of her friends said, "Ooooh, Jaymie."

Jamie turned, smiled, and waved at her. When we were out of sight, I pulled her close to me and kissed her again. This time our bodies were tight together. Her breast in her bathing suit rubbed against my naked chest. I untied the straps at the back of her neck. Now, we were flesh to flesh. We kissed again. I stiffened. In our embrace, she noticed. She touched me there, and I her. She surprised me when she said, "I want you," We removed our remaining clothing. She lay on the sand, and with a grace that amazed me, I penetrated her. I do not think she knew it was my first time.

When we returned to the little beach, the sun began setting. Her friends were gathering their things to leave.

"Good," one of her friends said, "I thought we were going to have to send out a search party to find you."

I walked her to their car. "Will you give me your phone number?"

"Yeah, sure." She asked the girl behind the wheel for something with which to write. She had nothing.

"Tell you what; I'll see you on campus. I'll give it to you then."

The next day was Saturday, and I did not get out of bed until the evening meal, and even then I felt hungover. I did not find Jamie. I began to have my doubts about her. I liked her. I found her sexy. I made love to her, but I didn't know her. *We made love! It must mean something? Is she my girl now? I don't know. Do I want her to be my girl? I don't know. Does she want me? I don't know.* I began to wish the whole thing would go away, and I wondered whether she wished it, too. A day or two later, I got my answer. When I saw her on campus, she pretended she didn't know me.

11

Sometimes I think we exist to make stories. Each life is one, and I wonder whether God reads them all or only the interesting ones. In my four years of college, my sophomore year was the least interesting. It just filled the gap between my freshman year and junior year, but the summer of that year changed America. The summer of 1967 is now called The Summer of Love.

College life had become routine. A freshman's insecurities grew into a relaxing familiarity. Jake and I were still roommates. Travis still lived across the hall. I rarely dated, but now, I had no excuse for not doing it. I had a car, bought with the money I saved from my summer job at my father's store. Did I mention my father owned a tuxedo rental company in downtown Atlanta?

The car I purchased was a 1963 beige Volkswagen Beetle. What else can I say about it? It was a Volkswagen Beetle and it was beige. They're all alike. Oh, yeah, it had a red interior.

I thought the car was pretty cool, but it was a different cool from the light blue 1964 GTO Travis brought to school. His car was badass cool. Mine was nerdy college cool. Jake brought his yellow 1953 Plymouth convertible, which in hindsight was the coolest car, but we didn't think so then. It was worn-out and needed refurbishing.

Like me, Jake rarely dated, but Travis dated several girls that year. I saw Marianne on campus sometimes. She said hello, but nothing more, which was an improvement from, "You aren't going to puke on me again, are you?" She still dated the same guy. A friend told me they were engaged. *Oh, well, so much for Snow White. Maybe she'll give birth to seven little dwarfs,* I thought.

Our sophomore year was the year men grew their hair long. The Beatles started it in 1964 with their shaggy haircuts, which looked as if the barber had cut their hair by putting a bowl on their heads and cutting around it. From that, men's hair grew longer and longer, but it had not grown to their shoulders yet. That came later. A man's politics could be judged by his hair, the longer the hair, the more liberal the politics. Jake's hair was longer than mine. His blond locks covered his ears. My hair covered only the top of mine. Travis did not change his hair style with the times. He wore it combed over as always.

The news about the war in Vietnam was like the beginning of a headache. The fall of our sophomore year was a time when you were not sure whether the slight pain in your head would grow into a serious headache or not. By the spring, it became a migraine.

The Vietnam War crept. At first, our government sent military advisers there, then thirty thousand troops, then a hundred, then a hundred and twenty-five-thousand. People supported the war, though most had never heard of Vietnam.

But when the casualties began coming home, people began questioning the war. The antiwar movement began with the radical far left who leaned toward the communists, but month by month it gained more supporters from regular Americans, especially after the Tet Offensive of 1968. We won the battle but America and its allies lost 3,470 men.

In the spring of our sophomore year, the war came to visit Jake and me.

I was lying on my bed when I heard the dorm room door open. Jake walked in, his eyes full of tears. Jake was a sensitive guy, but tough. I had seen him cry twice, once in a fight in high school when he was angered to tears as he beat up a bully who had teased him relentlessly, and once when his dog was run over by a delivery truck.

"What's wrong?" I asked.

"I just saw Danny." Danny was a high school classmate. He had news about two others in our class. "John is missing in action, and Eubanks is so shot up that he will probably never walk again."

Before, the war had been an ugly show on the nightly news. Now, it was real, too real. All young men who did not go to college or join the National Guard or Reserves were getting drafted, and there were no more openings in the Guard or Reserve units to avoid it. My brother's football knee injury became a blessing. He received a medical draft deferment. I could not be drafted while I was in college. My father assured me that the war would be over before I graduated, and I wondered if it was true, and I wondered how many more friends would be killed. Would I ever go?

Just before the end of spring quarter our sophomore year, Travis came to see Jake and me.

"You know that old country grocery store about a quarter-mile past the college on the right side of the road?"

"Yeah, Foster's Store. A bunch of basketball players live there, right?" Foster's Store was a country grocery store that had been converted to student housing.

"Exactly, they're not renting it next year. You guys want to get it?"

"Hell, yeah, that's a pretty cool place," Jake said.

That afternoon after class, we drove out to Foster's Store. Travis's friend, Jerry, gave us a tour.

Mr. Foster built the little country grocery store with concrete block. It had double doors and two four feet by four feet plate-glass windows, one on each side of the door. There were once gas pumps out front, but they had been removed, leaving the aluminum canopy. It was used as a porch now.

There was a small living room to the right as you entered a hall ahead, which led to a kitchen and a bath at the rear. It had one bedroom on the hall's left side and three on the right. The interior walls were the least expensive pine paneling money could buy. The kitchen fixtures were used, and the bathroom had a flimsy fiberglass shower. What more could a man want? We loved it.

We found Mr. Foster who lived next door. He was a ninety-three-year-old man who ran the grocery store until he retired at ninety. Now Mr. Foster operated a worm farm behind his house, night crawlers for fish bait. He told me that raising worms was more satisfying than the grocery business. I took him at his word.

"You boys want the place this fall?" he said.

"Yes, sir, we do," Travis said.

"Well, I will have to have a deposit."

"How much?" I asked.

"A month's rent in advance, thirty dollars from each of you, and that includes the fourth man. You got a fourth roommate?"

"No, sir, we'll find one," Travis said.

It took nearly all our money, but we did scrounge up enough. When I told my father about our plans, he looked skeptical. I eased his fears by telling him it would cost less than the dorm because we could cook our meals. I didn't believe what I told him, but as it happened, it was true.

That summer, I went back to Atlanta to work in my father's tux shop. I did not know then, but The Summer of Love approached, and I was right in the middle of what happened in Atlanta.

12

Jazz stood as the pinnacle of American music in the first half of the twentieth century. My parents and grandparents thought it would be America's favorite music forever, but by the early fifties it was staid and stale, or so avant garde that only musicians and the musically astute understood it.

In 1956, Elvis Presley sparked a revolution. He was a good-looking twenty-one-year old boy from Memphis who sang like a black man and wiggled like Little Egypt, making the teenage girls scream and run to the stage to touch him. Rock and roll was born. Our parents hated it, which fueled its popularity and caused a musical gap between the generations. America's youth had no idea the world watched their musical scene until the "fab four" came knocking on the door. The Beatles arrived, and the teenage girls screamed again. To our surprise, they sang our music, but with a British twist. Rock and roll had gone international.

At first the Beatles were fun, especially for the girls, but with the release of the "Sergeant Peppers" album their music spoke to us differently. The lighthearted "I Wanna Hold Your Hand" themes were replaced by deeper, more spiritual subjects. We didn't know then, but in the summer of 1967, America stood on the cusp of a revolution that defines our culture today.

Early in June after school had recessed for the summer, Jake and I were in his big yellow 1953 Plymouth convertible with the top down, driving on Atlanta's Peachtree Street on our way to the Fox theater to see "The Graduate."

"Listen to this," Jake said. He pulled an eight-track tape from a black case that sat between us on the seat. He inserted it in an eight-track tape player he had installed under his dashboard. As we drove, the tape player bounced up and down with every bump, but it worked.

Beatle Ringo played a drum beat, *boomp, chink, boomp, chink, boomp, boomp, chink,* overlaid with George Harrison's guitar riffs, and the Beatles sang,

It was twenty years ago today
Sergeant Peppers taught the band to play
They've been doing it in and out of style
But they're guaranteed to make you smile.

And they did make me smile. Each song related to the last song, but not overtly making one feel that there was a hidden story there.

"I wanna hear that again to see if I can figure out what they're getting at," I said. By now, Beatle John Lennon was singing, "*Ooooh, I get high with a little help from my friends.*"

"Well, that's pretty obvious what he's saying'," Jake said. "He's singing about smoking marijuana with his friends."

We had never seen any marijuana, but we knew that young people were smoking it in crazy places like California. I had read about it in *Life*.

"Listen to this." Jake punched a button on the eight-track several times. With each push the song changed until the Beatles sang, "*Lucy in the Sky with Diamonds. Lucy in the Sky with Diamonds.*"

"Lucy, sky, diamonds, think about it?" Jake said.

"LSD," I said. "Good God, this whole album is about drugs!" The *Life* article mentioned LSD, a hallucinatory drug also being used by the young Californians.

Traffic on Peachtree slowed. We thought there had been an accident. We crept forward until we came to a police barricade. A police officer directed us to turn right. Jake looked at him. With our top down, he could speak to us. "Gotta take West Peachtree. The hippies have Peachtree blocked at Tenth." Jake made the turn, then looked at me. "What's a hippie?"

"A hippie is like a beatnik but younger, and he listens to rock instead of jazz, and he has long hair like the Beatles. Girl hippies wear baggy dresses, put flowers in their hair, and don't wear bras," is how I answered his question that night. The hippies had also been in the *Life* article. They had taken over a neighborhood in San Francisco called Haight-Ashbury, but I had no idea the same thing was happening in Atlanta.

"Don't wear bras! That ought to be fun. Damn the movie. Let's park, and go up there and see what's going on." We parked and walked up to Peachtree.

In hindsight, it was inevitable. The timing was perfect. World War II had ended twenty-two years earlier. The baby boomers were growing up. In 1967, America had a disproportionate number of young adults, too many to ignore, and we impacted the culture, and we made all the mistakes common to the young. I was in front of the wave, blindly stumbling into the new world.

Hippies filled Peachtree Street in their "anything goes" clothes, bellbottom jeans, colorful shirts and dresses, headbands and leathers. They walked in the street and on the sidewalk and in and out of shops. In standard dress like Jake and me, the less hip were there also to look at "the scene" as everyone called it.

A few months before, I had driven on this part of Peachtree, and it looked as it always looked. Now the shops sold bellbottom jeans, brightly-colored shirts, vests, beaded headbands, leather jackets, and purses with long leather fringes, and long dresses that looked like those of a Gypsy fortune-teller. There were art shops and poster shops with black-light posters, head shops, and record shops which carried the latest psychedelic music, and there were clubs with folk or rock music.

Jake pointed to a poster, "Look, wanna go?"

The poster said a band we did not know, called The Allman Brothers, were giving a free concert in Piedmont Park.

"I don't know. Maybe. I wonder if they are any good."

I could tell Jake liked what he saw as we walked. He stopped, turned to me, and said, "Groovy" in his hippest slang.

I replied, "Outa sight," in mine.

But suddenly, I began to feel square in my plaid madras shirt, khaki pants, and Weeguns. "Let's go get one of those T-shirts with all the colors, I keep seeing around." We did not know they were called tie-dyed T-shirts then, but we found some and changed shirts right in the store, something you could not do at Rich's where I bought most of my clothes. *Now we're cool.*

We walked down Fourteenth Street toward Piedmont Park. Apartment buildings lined the street. Some windows glowed violet with black light, and as we walked, music from open apartment windows surrounded us.

"Listen," Jake said. "It's Hendrix."

Purple haze all in my brain
Lately things don't seem the same
Actin' funny and I don't know why
Excuse me while I kiss the sky

Jimi Hendrix's voice carried from the building to the sidewalk. "Do you think purple haze is some kinda drug?" Jake asked.

"I don't know. Probably," I said.

As we walked, we heard The Doors, Steppenwolf, Janice Joplin, The Who, and The Rolling Stones leaking through open windows.

"What's that smell," Jake asked. We stood below an open apartment window with a black light's glow coming from it.

"I think we smell smoke from a marijuana cigarette,"

"Really?"

The next morning at breakfast, my father read the newspaper while I ate. He folded the paper and laid it on the table where I could see the headline. "Look at this," he said as he pointed to the paper.

"Youth Block Peachtree Street. Drug Use Suspected," it said.

"I'm glad you weren't there."

Before I could comment, the phone rang. I answered it. Jake spoke. "Hey, man, Simmons called. He has rented a house on Juniper between Tenth and Fourteenth right in the middle of the action. He's having a party. He invited us."

"Groovy," I said. We chatted for a few minutes, then he hung up.

"What's that you were saying, Dad?"

"It's not important. Come on, let's get to work."

13

Later, when I could get some privacy, I called Jake.
"Simmons called late. He saw us in the crowd but
lost us. He and two other Tech guys have rented one
of those old houses on Juniper. They're havin' a
party Friday night and we're invited."

"Is it a hippie party?" I asked.

"Well, it ain't a church social."

"What are you wearing?"

"You sound like a girl. I don't know. I guess
I'll wear that tee-shirt we bought and some jeans."

"If I wear mine, we'll look like the Bobbsey
Twins, so I'm gonna buy something. All my other
clothes are too square."

"Now, you really do sound like a girl."

I don't like shopping and put it off until Friday after work. From Greenbrier Mall where I planned to shop, I was going to Jake's house. We were driving to Simmons' place in his car from there.

I grew up in the men's clothing industry. My father and grandfather were men who always carried a cloth measuring tape in their pocket, if not hanging around their necks. My grandfather opened a men's shop back in 1918, but by my time, it had become a tuxedo rental company.

In those days, grown men with families sold men's clothing in department stores and men's shops like Muse's and Zachary's. We didn't know then, but we were in the end of an era. Men's clothiers would soon be obsolete as clever marketing companies replaced expertise with low paid youths in the emerging shopping mall culture.

Sergeant Pepper's, a new type store, opened in Greenbrier Mall, not far from my house. It offered a good selection of hip goods, bellbottom jeans, vests, shirts, and accessories. Shopping at Sergeant Peppers was a new experience for me.

Rock music played in the background there. Most stores did not have music in those days. If they did, it would be calming, designed to lull you into buying something.

Posters of rock stars hung on the walls and glowed under black lights. A young man about my age approached me. "Hey, man, what's happening," he said instead of the traditional, "May I help you?" He wore bellbottom jeans, a black leather vest over a white shirt with an exaggerated collar. His shirt's three top buttons were unbuttoned. Dark hair covered his ears and he had a long mustache. His looks alone could have gotten him fired at Rich's.

I told him what I needed, and he fixed me up with a sack full of hip but shoddy goods.

"I'm pressed for time. You care if I put these things on in your dressing room?" I asked.

"Of course, not."

I put on my new bell bottom jeans, a collarless, fake linen, V-neck pullover with butterflies embroidered around the neck, and a leather vest with long leather fringe. I swapped my brown, Florsheim tassel loafers for some cheap, Italian-looking, high heel boots. I bought accessories, too a hounds tooth go-go hat like I had seen Bob Dylan wearing and some round sunglasses as I had seen on Beatle John Lennon. I looked at my watch. I was late.

The clunk of the hard heels of my fake Italian boots hitting the mall's tile floor echoed as I walked -- clunk, clunk. I rounded a corner and collided with a girl. There stumbling off balance stood Snow White. She grabbed the wall to balance herself.

"Good God, Rick, first you throw up on me, then you knock me over. You're a walking disaster."

"I'm sorry, Marianne... Auh, I wasn't expecting to run into you here. . . a, a away from school, I mean...."

"I wasn't expecting you to run into me, a, a away from school either, but somehow, I'm not surprised. Why are you dressed like that?"

"I'm going to a party. It's the latest style." I stepped back to model for her.

"It is?" she said.

"It is," I repeated.

"Well, okay! Have fun at the party!" She walked away, then clunk, clunk, I walked away, too. Because I liked the way she looked, I turned to get one more glimpse of her. She also turned, and she had a big smile on her face. She laughed. *Maybe she likes me after all,* I thought, clunk, clunk, clunk.

Ten minutes later, Jake and I were in his car headed for the party. "Rick," he said.

"What?'

"You've still got a big tag on your hat. Why don't you ditch the hat and the glasses? It just ain't you, buddy."

"You think it's too much?"

"You look like you are trying too hard." I threw them in the back seat. "The vest too, you can wear it later." I did the same with the vest.

"That's better."

"Maybe I got a little carried away in the store."

"I think you did. I like the shirt and pants though," Jake said.

It took a half-hour to drive to Simmons' house. That's fast for Atlanta. Traffic was light. His house was a two-story Victorian with a steep roof, a turret on the left side and a porch across the front. A two-foot high black garden fence made from ornamental iron rod arches joined one to another surrounded the front yard. At the walkway, a gate stood open. The shrubs and yard were unkept and the house needed painting. The city had rezoned the street commercial, and probably a real-estate speculator who did not want to invest in improvements owned it.

"This place would make a great haunted house if it were out on a lonely road," Jake said as we walked up the four steps to the front porch.

The front door loomed over us nine feet tall, made of mahogany with a glass panel in it. The panel was covered by pleated sheers stretched over the glass so you could not see in. A brass mechanical doorbell sat in the middle of the door. When I twisted the handle, it sounded like a bicycle bell.

Fingers pulled the sheers back. An eye appeared in the gap, and someone said, "It's okay. They're cool." Two locks clicked then the door opened. The eye belonged to Simmons. "Hey, hey," he said, "Come on in and meet everybody. You already know some of them."

We walked in, and with the steps, we walked from the well-ordered world of our childhood to the chaos that claimed then next ten years as America reinvented itself.

14

Our eyes filled with a dark living room lit by a black light's glow. Simmons closed and locked the door. The well-worn furniture sat unused. Instead, all sat on a large oriental rug, which lay in the center of the living-room floor. Six young women and four young men sat in a circle, some reclining on oversize throw pillows, passing a joint.

"What's up, Rick, Jake?" one guy said as he drew in a big breath of smoke. I did not recognize the face, but his voice sounded familiar. He wore a beard, and he wore his hair long, but who. . . . Finally, he breathed. "It's me, Bishop."

"Bishop! Good God almighty, last time I saw you, you had a flattop."

Another guy from the group stood. "Who am I?" He too wore a beard.

I studied his face. "Chuck?"

"Right." He gave me a hug as if I were a lost dog come home.

Simmons introduced the others. Most, but not all the girls, were paired with one of the guys. One called herself Skylark. Simmons said she was an artist, and a Dylan song began playing in my head:

> *She's got everything she needs*
> *She's an artist, she don't look back-*

I joined the circle, choosing to sit next to Skylark, and I noticed she looked pleased. The Dylan song still played in my head, but my ears heard Jefferson Airplane's Grace Slick singing from the speakers of an expensive looking stereo:

> *One pill makes you larger*
> *And one pill makes you small*
> *And the ones that mother gives you*
> *Don't do anything at all.*
> *Go ask Alice when she is ten feet tall.*

Everything around me, Skylark's beauty, Dylan, the marijuana smell in the room, old and new friends, the Jefferson Airplane, the black light and the black-light posters taped to the walls, made me high before the joint they passed got to me. It was two people away. Now it was my turn. I inhaled it as if it were a tobacco cigarette. Skylark laughed. "Let me show you." She drew smoke into her lungs and held it for as long as she could. I did the same.

"Oh, wow," seems the usual response to one's first taste of marijuana, and I had the same reaction. I lay back on one of the large throw pillows. Skylark sat beside me, looking at me. Her braless breast peeked through the thin fabric of her white tunic. Her brown hair hung over them, sometimes obstructing a pleasant view. I relaxed. I had gotten high, and I wanted her. We talked, but it was a formality. Even in my sexual inexperience, I knew I was chosen. I saw I would spend the night with her, and I did. When I awoke next morning, she was gone. I found Simmons' sitting on his front porch smoking a cigarette.

"About Skylark," he said.

"What about her?"

"Skylark is not her real name. It's Debby Morton. She's a great artist but, how can I put this . . . She is an artist . . . what else do I need to say? If you start caring about her, you are going to get yourself hurt. When it comes to men, she has the attention span of a gnat."

"Got it."

He took another long draw off his cigarette, then looked at me, "Was it good?"

"Hell, yeah, great," I said. I thought of her scent, the shape of her breast, the way they moved as she sat astride me, the way her body tensed, the way she leaned forward and kissed me at the right moment, the way she wanted more, then more. I remembered the rest of the Dylan song stuck in my head the night before:

> *You will start out standing*
> *Proud to steal her anything she needs*
> *But you will end up peeking through a key*
hole
> *Down upon your knees.*

The lyrics fit, but I wasn't going to let myself end up "down upon my knees." And I remembered something my father once said. Perhaps, it was the best advice he ever gave me, "Never live it up, so you can't live it down."

Simmons was a big blond guy, a strong tackle on our high school football team. In high school, he wore a football player's buzzed haircut, but now, his shoulder-length hair grew longer than any male I knew.

Simmons was smart, smart enough to get a scholarship to Georgia Tech, and that's smart, especially when you consider Georgia Tech draws good students from all over the world. It was on summer break. Simmons was not in school or working. I wondered if he could give up this perpetual party when fall quarter came, or would he try to keep this way of life and study at the same time. I knew I couldn't do it. I would have to walk away or succumb, but I could not do both. I feared Simmons had "lived it up, so he couldn't live it down." Time would tell.

Jake stumbled on to the porch. "Sleep good?" I asked.

"No. You were driving me crazy." He looked at Simmons. "Have you ever tried to sleep while your best buddy is getting laid in the room next door? It's horrible." He returned his gaze to me. "What were you doing in there, moving furniture? Every time I thought you had finished, you'd start again. I was fucking jealous, I could hardly stand it. That Skylark, she's a real moaner; isn't she?"

"What happened to Jan? She was the other single girl at the party.

"I blew it. That's what happened. I don't want to talk about it."

"If you guys can hang around, I'll rustle up some breakfast, then give you the grand tour of the strip."

"Sounds good," Jake said. I agreed. . . .

15

After breakfast we walked to Peachtree Street. The sun rose at six. By now the clock read eight. Everything looked grey, but it wasn't foggy. The grey mood was felt more than seen, the same hollow feeling one has after a wild party, finding a room filled with empty beer cans, half-full glasses, and full ashtrays, and yourself with a hangover. Night people move slowly in the morning if they move at all.

A black man pushed a big galvanized mop bucket with a wringer on it through a closed bar's open door. He held the mop's handle, the mop being submerged in the bucket. He emptied it in the gutter, locked the door and loaded his old pickup. He was a morning person. I forget the bar's name, but painted on the window was a cartoon of a man walking. "Keep on Trucking" was written below the man. I thought it funny, but not sure why.

On the corner of Tenth and Peachtree, a bearded young man dressed in an olive drab shirt that looked like something salvaged from the army of an eastern bloc country, sold roses to those who passed. When the light turned red, he stepped into the street with his box of roses, using sentences with the words "peace" and "love" in them to make a sale. When we walked by, he said, "Peace, Brother."

I made the V shaped peace sign with my fingers and returned the greeting. He did not look at peace to me as he nervously rubbed at his arms like Ray Charles did when I saw him in concert. I wondered why then. I now know it is a sign of heroin addiction.

"Isn't this great!" Simmons said, "Come here. I wanna show you a store. It hasn't opened yet, but we can look through the window."

We walked to the Merry-go-Round. "Look in here. If the establishment doesn't like it, they got it," he said. What he said was true. Their stock made the mall store where I shopped the day before look like a Savile Row tailor shop in London. Whatever society considered inappropriate, the Merry-go-

Round carried, from spike collars to the latest in cross-dresser fashions.

When we reached Fourteenth, Simmons said, "I wanna show you this place." We turned to the right on Fourteenth and walked a few feet. He pointed to a door that led to a basement. The sign by the door said, "Catacombs," and a yellow and orange poster announced, "Playing Tonight–Bag." A black-and-white picture of the band was printed on it. I had never heard of Bag, but Simmons said, "They're outta sight."

"It's a crazy place. The other night two guys in leather spiked collars handcuffed themselves together all night. They were in love or something, and girls kiss girls all the time in there. The place stays packed. People sit on the floor," Simmons said.

I peeked in the window and saw a basement bar room, with pipes hanging from the ceiling.

"Cool," I said.

"Come on," Simmons said. "We'll go see my friend Marie; she owns a head shop. She should be open by now."

"What's a head shop?" Jake asked. I wished he hadn't asked that question. I didn't know either, but would have played along until we found out. The question made us look naive, which we were, but I didn't want to advertise it even to Simmons.

"You'll see," Simmons said in answer to Jake's question. We continued our walk.

"Here's Marie's biggest competitor," he said as we walked past a shop called the Morning Glory Seed. Then I heard a drum. The sound was not the *boom chink* of an American drummer, but the *boing, boing* of an East Indian one. Then I heard chanting, "Hare Krishna, Hare Krishna, Hare Krishna, Hare Krishna." And then I saw them standing on the corner down the street. They wore what I thought was orange bed sheets. Their heads were shaved except for a pigtail that hung from the center of the back of their head to their shoulders. To my surprise, they were Caucasian Americans, not East Indians as I first thought. "I hate those stupid assholes," Simmons said as we passed, Krishna, Hare Krishna, Hare Krishna, boing, boing, Hare Krishna. "You are not your body. Take a pamphlet." He poked a pamphlet at Simmons. The chant Hare Krishna and the drum continued, Hare Krishna, boing, boing. "Would you like to make a donation?" one asked.

"Oh, fuck you," Simmons said.

Hmm, you are not your body? I agree with that, I thought as we walked by. A few years later, The Beatles' George Harrison would record "My

Sweet Lord," in which the background singers would sing Hare Krishna repeatedly. The Beatles had recently returned to England from India where they studied with a guru. The Indian influence can be heard in their music, especially the "Sergeant Peppers" album. If The Beatles said Eastern thought was cool, then it was cool. That's how much influence they had over the culture back then.

We arrived at Marie's. The sign above the door read, "Marie's Potted Plant Emporium." But there were no potted plants. Marie sat on the sidewalk in front of her store. She wore an earthy, brown, bare shoulder, long, hippie dress and no shoes. Her feet were the dirtiest I had ever seen. Her brown hair hung over her shoulders, and her armpits were hairy; even so, she was appealing, and frightening at the same time, and unforgettable. She smelled like patchouli incense or perhaps patchouli perfume, everything on the strip smelled like patchouli or sandalwood to me.

"What's up, Marie?" Simmons said.

"Not much. Who are your friends?"

"This is Jake and this is Rick."

"You guys newbies or sightseers?" she asked.

"I don't know, what's the difference?" I said.

"A newbie is new to our community. A sightseer is exactly what it sounds like it is, someone who is here to see the sights."

"I guess we are sightseers then. We're home from college for the summer."

"Mind if we look around," Simmons asked.

"Go ahead. That's what I am here for."

Jake and I had never seen goods like hers. She sold every type of bong, hookah, and pipe imaginable. Some looked like glass contraptions I used in the Chemistry Lab back at West Georgia. She carried a selection of black light posters and the black lights to go with them, hippie art and jewelry, even small rugs. I bought a copy of *The Great Speckled Bird*, an underground newspaper, but I did not read it till later.

We joined Marie on the sidewalk and made small talk until Simmons said, "Oh, shit, here comes that Jesus freak, Paul."

"I like him," Marie said.

"I don't like any Jesus freak, and I don't like those Hare Krishna assholes either. Only dumbasses believe in God," Simmons said.

"I agree," Jake said.

Jake surprised me. We never discussed religion. I knew he grew up a Baptist, and I knew like most young people he wasn't religious. Neither was I, but I assumed his beliefs were something similar to mine.

Paul joined the group. He wore his hair long, but he dressed neatly. He was a few years older than the rest of us. I liked him immediately, but felt standoffish. I am never sure how to act around preachers, especially ones close to my age. I don't want them to discover what a heathen I am, but I gotta believe, what I believe, the way I believe it. Anything else would be a lie, to them and me. On the other hand, I am not that bad.

"Where you headed?" Marie asked Paul.

"The Twelfth Gate," Paul said. The Twelfth Gate was a coffee shop operated by the Methodist Church.

"Saved anybody's ass lately, Paul?" Simmons said as though the question was part of an earlier conversation to which I had not been privy.

"No, Simmons, I haven't saved anybody's ass lately, a soul or two, but not an ass."

Simmons' voice angered. "What makes you think you can save anybody's anything?"

"I can't save anybody, but I know who can."

"Bullshit, you Christians do more harm than good.

"How many have you killed in the name of Jesus?

"Simmons, I've told you before. Anyone can kill in the name of Jesus. That doesn't mean that Jesus sanctioned it. The fact they did it means they didn't follow his teachings. He preached peace, love, and understanding long before you hippies did."

"All you preachers want is money. You want to get inside my wallet, but I've . . . been inside God, man. I took a trip and saw God. I've seen his love firsthand."

"No, Simmons, what you saw on your acid trip wasn't God. Sorry, that's different."

"How would you know where I've been? How would you know what I saw?"

"You're right; I don't know what you saw. I do know it wasn't real."

He turned to Marie. "Now, if you will excuse me, I must go. Nice to see you again, Marie, and you too Simmons." He nodded toward Jake and me, "Fellows," he said, then continued his walk.

After he was gone, Simmons said, "I can't stand that self-righteous, know it all, Jesus-freak." Simmons' hostility surprised me.

"What a jerk-off," Jake said.

Jake surprised me as well. I thought Simmons had been rude and for no reason, *live and let live.*

Later in the mid-nineteen-eighties, I would see Paul and Marie again. Paul would be the pastor of a large church in Atlanta, and when I knew Marie later in life, she had become a Jaguar driving, Jones of New York business suit wearing, owner of a real estate agency. No one would guess she was a hippie, but when you think about it, it is not as farfetched as it seems. She was a business woman when she was a hippie, and she is still a business woman. In both cases, she dressed to fit the role. She changed to fit the times.

On our way home, Jake drove while I read The *Great Speckled Bird* aloud to him. I read one article about how President Johnson profited from the Vietnam War, and one about marijuana smoke being good for you. I didn't like the war, but I didn't think Johnson was so uncaring that he would start a war just to make a buck, and I didn't think any smoke in your lungs was good for you, marijuana, tobacco, or a house fire. *Marijuana may be fun, but it can't be good for your lungs,* I thought, but I didn't say it then. Saying something like that was uncool and to a young man in 1967, it was more important to be cool than to be right.

16

Jake had been my best friend all my life. I was Batman. He was Robin. At least, that is the way I saw it. To him the roles may have been reversed. Either way we were close. Most summers I took two vacations, one with my family and one with his. He got two as well.

We didn't do everything together for the first time in the summer of 1967. My father needed me to work in his tuxedo rental business that summer. Jake spent his time with Simmons. I joined them when I could.

Dad supplied rental tuxedos to men's shops throughout the Southeast and to locals in Atlanta. We weren't rich, but we were comfortable. From the time I was ten, I accompanied my father to work on Saturdays. I can see now that it was a ploy to give my mother a break, but by the time I turned fourteen, I was a good worker.

I met Jake one evening for burgers at the Varsity, an Atlanta icon. It is called the world's largest drive-in restaurant, and that is easy to believe. It seats eight-hundred, and can park six-hundred cars. Made from tan and maroon porcelain panels like an old gas station, its art deco architecture is a throwback to an earlier time. The Varsity has been in business since 1928 and is part of Atlanta's personality. When it opened, it sat on the outer edge of Atlanta but the city had grown around it. I wandered through the crowd until I found Jake sitting at a table in a part called the bridge which connects the restaurant building to the parking lot's second story.

"Over here," he said, waving his hand. We jumped into a line and ordered. We ate in one of several dining rooms, all with TVs on the wall tuned to one of the three networks. The picture showed the coffins of soldiers returning from Vietnam being unloaded from an airplane somewhere. Jake and I paid no attention. After a few minutes into our conversation, Jake said, "Simmons wants us to try acid." By acid, I knew he meant LSD. I stopped eating.

"You can do it if you want, but I'm not."

"Why?"

"Because, Art Linkletter's daughter jumped off a high-rise's window thinking she could fly while on an acid trip." Art Linkletter was a much-loved TV talk show host. "Crap like that happens all the time and too many go on acid trips and never come back. I'm not spending the rest of my life in Milledgeville." By Milledgeville, I meant the state mental institution there. "That's why. It's not worth the risk for a few minutes fun to me."

Jake looked disappointed. "I thought we . . . never mind." I knew then he would do it. Simmons told him that it would expand his mind. Jake wanted that. I liked my mind the way it was. Later, Jake told me about his acid trip. He giggled as he talked about it.

"It was cool, man, he-he. Simmons gave me this stamp to lick. The Mad Hatter was printed on it. Get it, the Mad Hatter, he-he-he."

"Yeah, I get it, the Mad Hatter."

"At first, nothing happened. Then I looked at the clock, man, and it was sort of like bent out of shape. Sort of like that Salvador Dali painting but not that much." He giggled again. "And then the colors came. You wouldn't believe the colors, man. And then . . . and then Simmons' eyeballs melted and ran down his face." He giggled some more. "It was cool, man."

"Did you see God like Simmons did?"

"Well, not exactly."

"That's what I thought. I'm not doing it, man." I emphasized the word man, mocking his overuse of hip talk. I'll stick with beer and maybe a little pot now and then, man."

Jake and I always agreed on everything, but on that day for the first time, I could see us taking different tacks; even so, I loved him.

Later in our conversation, I told Jake that I didn't see how Simmons could keep partying and keep his grades up at Georgia Tech.

"Simmons is really, really smart. You know that. He can do it. He'll graduate all right."

Jake got it right. Simmons did graduate from Georgia Tech, ten years later and after two stays in rehab. Cool has a price. *Never live it up, so you can't live it down.*

Summer ended, Jake, Travis and I made plans for our move into Foster's Store.

17

I recently drove an old Volkswagen Beatle on the Interstate, a frightening experience to say the least. The car is so slow that you can barely go fast enough to keep from being bounced around like the steel ball in a pinball machine. Back in 1967, the Volkswagen felt comfortable to me as I drove on Highway 166 from my part of Atlanta to Carrollton. I took corners like a race car driver, downshifted at the right places, braked before I entered a turn so I could take it at top speed. I pushed the car to its maximum, and barely broke the speed limit. I could have fun without getting a ticket.

Travis couldn't say the same about his GTO. It could go more than twice the legal limit. Even Jake's fifty-three Plymouth could get you in trouble.

We were moving into Foster's Store. My entire net worth sat in the Beatle's backseat and trunk and it wasn't full. Just to see what was happening, I drove through the campus. When I returned to Maple Street, I turned right and began shifting through all four gears. As I reached fourth, I saw Foster's Store ahead; I downshifted back to third, *brooooom*, then to second, *brooooom* again. I did this countless times during my stay at Foster's.

Travis parked by the front door under the canopy that once covered the gas pumps. Jake parked behind him. I parked by Jake and began unloading.

Mr. Foster provided beds, a dresser, and a small desk in each bedroom. He also provided a sofa for the living room, and a dining table and chairs in the kitchen. Travis brought an overstuffed chair his parents no longer wanted, and Jake brought the black-and-white TV we bought at a pawn shop for only ten bucks.

The furniture sat in place, now to decorate. Neon beer signs, of course, we were college boys after all. Travis brought two. One read Pabst Blue Ribbon, and the other read Miller High Life with a neon girl sitting on a neon half-moon. I hung two posters. One of King Kong clinging to the Empire State Building, which we thought funny, and another of poet Allen Ginsburg sitting on a toilet with the caption. "The job ain't finished until the paperwork is done." We thought that funny, too.

Mr. Foster had replaced the toilet over the summer, and the old one sat out front. I bought a rubber tree plant and a bag of potting soil and used the old toilet as a planter for it. Travis, the only one of us who regularly needed contraception, provided Trojans, which he Scotch taped to the rubber tree making it look . . . well, you know.

To top off the decorations, Jake attached an unused chair upside down to the ceiling, I thought our place should be in *Better Homes and Gardens*, but *Mad Magazine* might have been a better choice.

We sat in the living room toasting our handiwork with a beer, when the front door opened without warning and a man with a hand truck loaded with ice-cream came walking in. He got down the hall before he realized something was wrong. "Hey," he said, "This ain't a store."

"I know," Travis said, as if surprised by the fact.

"Did you boys order this ice cream?"

"No, sir, I don't know anything about it."

"Well, I'll be. . ." He walked out cursing.

People walked in regularly, thinking it still a store. Evidently, Mr. Foster had an old Coca-Cola drink box which he filled with soft drinks and ice. People remembered that Foster's Store had the coldest drinks in town. "No, not anymore," I told them. "Mr. Foster is in the worm business now."

Later that afternoon, Tony, our fourth housemate, showed up. Jake and I recruited him over the summer. He transferred from Georgia State in Atlanta. Tony was in the class behind Jake and me at Therrell High. He was smart and he was tough. I saw him fight. He was losing. His nose was flattened, but he wouldn't give up, so I knew how tough he was, but I didn't realize how smart he was then. He made A's in high school without cracking a book. No one thought to put Tony on a list of smart kids at our high school, except his teachers. He didn't look or act the part.

Tony stood five-nine with a medium build and dirty blond hair. I didn't think him particularly handsome, nor did I think him unattractive. I liked him. Like Jake, Travis and me, he liked to have a good time. I knew he would fit in.

He showed up in a '64 GTO like Travis' save for the color. Tony's painted white. Travis's painted blue. Both cars had black interiors. It was a used car but new to him. We went out to look at it.

"Is yours a 389?" Travis asked.

"Yep," Tony said.

"Four-speed transmission?"

"Yep."

"Run good?"

"Like a scalded dog," Tony said.

"Mine, too," Travis said.

Sooner or later there will be a race, I thought. We stepped away from the cars.

"Anybody know who lives in the house down the hill?" Jake asked.

Mr. Foster owned a concrete-block house down the hill behind the store. The house was in bad shape, worn-out linoleum flooring, leaky casement window, gas room heaters that had to be lit with a match, but what do you want for thirty dollars a month. That was cheap even then.

"I haven't got the slightest idea who is living there. Let's go see," Travis said. We walked down to it, and knocked on the door. A friend from Strozier Hall answered our knock.

Travis looked, "Walter."

"Come on in, guys," he said.

We walked in, "Who else lives here?"

"Craver and Abernathy." All were friends from Strozier Hall.

Jake looked at me, then we looked at Travis, then we looked at Walter, and a smile came to our faces.

"Party time!" Travis said.

At a little college with little to do, in a little town also with little to do, the news about a party spreads at exactly the speed of sound. Throw in a keg of beer and the news travels at twice the speed of sound. "Did you hear? Keg party at Foster's Store."

"No, shit! I'll be there."

In those days, the wooded area between Foster's Store and today's CVS pharmacy was a pasture. Yes, as I write this, Fosters Store is still standing, though barely. The night of the party, the pasture became our parking lot. Other times we used it as a football field.

That night, Tony's expensive stereo blasted out, Carla Thomas and Otis Redding in a musical conversation:

"Tramp," sang Carla.

"What'd you say?" sang Otis.

"Tramp."

"Ooooh, I'm a lover. I'm a lover," Otis sang.

Gink, gink, gink, gink went the guitar.

Soul music was still the favorite at West Georgia in the fall of 1967, especially for parties. We danced. We drank beer mostly, but out in the pasture, Jake and some new friends listened to *In-a-Gagda-Divida,* the most psychedelic of psychedelic music, on someone's car eight-track, while they sat in a circle and passed a joint.

Boring, I thought. *Why do that when I can drink beer and dance with a pretty girl?* And I drank beer, and I danced with every girl who would dance with me, so did Travis.

The September night felt warm, the sky clear and the moon was full. Foster's Store vibrated with people and music. We had no idea so many would come. I worried the police might come as well. Had we been closer to town, I am sure they would have. I danced as Aretha Franklin sang, "R E S P E C T, find out what it means to me," and I drank from the keg we bought.

Wilson Pickett sang, "Mustang Sally, huh, you had better slow that Mustang down," when Marianne came in with her boyfriend, the squeaky-clean letter-sweater-wearing, MG driving doofus. As I danced, I watched them. He looked lost. I could easily imagine them parked in a lover's lane somewhere listening to The Lettermen, the squarest of all square musical groups then. I assumed he liked them since he always wore a letter sweater. He was two years older and knew no one at the party. He looked at Marianne with, "Honey, let's go" eyes. But Marianne's eyes said, "Go away, and let me have a good time." He got his way. They didn't hang around long.

"Stay" by Maurice Williams and the Zodiacs was the last song Tony played. Most left when the music stopped, but a few drunken guys slept on the couch or floor until the early morning.

I awoke at eleven the next morning with a premonition. *My parents are coming.* I woke Jake, Travis, and Tony.

"How do you know?" Travis asked.

"I don't know how I know. I just know." Somehow, I convinced them I was right. Despite our hangovers, we got out of bed and cleaned up the mess from the party, then sprayed air freshener to cover the cigarette smell.

I was right. At exactly one-thirty, they knocked on the door, and we answered it as good boys should. . . .

18

It must have been a Saturday. I do not recall where my housemates had gone, but I stood alone, at the kitchen sink washing dishes and looking out the window. I could see Mr. Foster with a hoe, doing whatever one does to make earth worms grow. I suppose he fed them earthworm food, whatever that is.

He wore a khaki shirt and pants with a gray felt fedora hat atop his head. The hat and the shirt were soaked through with sweat. *That's mighty hard work for a ninety-three-year-old man,* I thought. I did some quick math. He was born in 1874. *That's nine years after the Civil War ended. If he lived in the country, he was probably fifty before he had electricity. He may have been thirty-five before he learned to drive a car. No doubt, he knows more about horses than cars, kerosene lamps than electric ones.* Mr. Foster made me feel connected to history, and I liked that.

In a few minutes, he knocked on my door. His khaki shirt was buttoned to the top, which made him look old-fashioned, but when you are ninety-three it is impossible to not look old-fashioned.

"Whew," he said. "It's mighty hot out there."

"Yes, sir, Mr. Foster, It's a hot one all right. Don't you think you ought to take it easy working your worms?"

"Them worms is what keeps me alive. I get exercise foolin' with them, and they give me something to think about. Say, I was wondering, could I have one of those beers I see you boys runnin' around with. I'm mighty hot."

"Sure, Mr. Foster, I'll get you one." I went to the refrigerator and got a Pabst Blue Ribbon for him. He opened it and took a sip.

"Thank you. I appreciate it. Which one of them little gals I see runnin' around here is your girlfriend."

"None of 'um, Mr. Foster, I don't have a girlfriend."

"Don't have a girlfriend! Why a good-looking boy like you ought to have a girlfriend. There is a yard full of girls down at the school. Go down there and get you one."

He's right! I ain't so bad. Why don't I have a girlfriend? He makes it sound so easy. Go down there and get you one.

We at Foster's Store always watched the evening news. Young men like us were dying in Vietnam. The war wouldn't go away, and the other stories in the news were bad as well. Racial unrest, cities burning, and war protests attacked our eyes every night. To escape the ugliness, we watched *The Andy Griffith Show* and *Gilligan's Island,* but the stations in Atlanta were a long distance away and our TV had a snowy picture. I hoped to improve it by moving the antenna from the roof to high in a tree.

I collapsed the antenna and tied it to my belt, and climbed the tree with the cable, already attached to it, hanging behind me. I was nailing a bracket to the tree when I heard soft feminine tones with a southern accent.

"Boy, what are you doing in a tree?"

"Who me?"

"Well, I don't see anyone else in a tree. Do you?"

"Auh, I'm moving our TV antenna." We could not see each other for the foliage. "Can I help you with something?"

"Is Tony here?"

"Not right now."

"Rats."

"You here for the book?" Tony had given me a copy of "Moby Dick" to give to a girl in his English Literature class should she come by while he was away.

"Yes."

"Hold on, I've got it." I laid the antenna across some branches, and climbed down, still unable to see the girl. I jumped off the lowest branch squarely in front of her."

"Oh," she said. "It's you. Are you drunk again? You aren't going to throw up on me again are you?"

"Marianne!" *My God, it's Marianne.* My pulse pounded. I took a breath.

"No. I'll tell you what. You throw up on me, and we will be even."

"I do not feel the need to do that, Mr. Rinehart." Her voice was polite yet playful.

"Mr. Rinehart, students don't address each other like that."

"I do not feel the need to be familiar with you, Mr. Rinehart."

Familiar, I feel the need to get familiar with you, real familiar.

"Where is your boyfriend?" Her voice became lower in pitch. "I sent his ass back to Buckhead where he belongs." She smiled, brushed her hair back with her hand. "Come here, you've got leaves all over your shoulders." I stepped forward, and she brushed them off. "Now where's that book?"

She likes me. If that's not flirting, I don't know what is!

"Damn the book. Let's go to dinner," I said.

"But it's four o'clock."

"Let's do it anyway."

"But I'm supposed to read *Moby Dick*."

"Do you always do what you are supposed to?"

"Always."

"Yah, sure."

"Well, I am a little hungry."

As far as I know, the Pizza Palace was Carrollton's first pizzeria and the only restaurant in town with anything near a romantic ambience. No doubt, this meal should be at the Pizza Palace.

The restaurant had just opened for dinner. We were the only customers. Waiters hurried distributing condiments to tables. The background music began to play, Sinatra. Italians love Ole Blue Eyes. The meal was simple. We shared a pizza and Cokes. I have eaten many pizzas over the years, but because of her, this pizza tasted the best of all. We talked and we flirted with our eyes and our hands touched.

On my tenth birthday, I saw the Disney classic movie *Lady and the Tramp*. Though I didn't admit it to the other boys, when the Tramp and the Lady found themselves on the same spaghetti strand and their lips met, I cried. That was more than I could hope for on this night, but we did have our *Lady and the Tramp* moments with looks, the touching of hands and a kiss, and then another. And we talked while I drove her back to Adamson Hall. I parked, and we talked more.

I learned that her father worked at Delta as a pilot and owned a gentleman's farm in Brooks where she grew up. Marianne had horses. I asked about her boyfriend.

"Boring," she said. "All he wanted to do was make out, and he wasn't even any good at that. My mom liked him. She's mad with me for breaking up."

She pointed to a window in Adamson Hall. "That's my room right there," she said.

I put my arm around her, and she pulled to me, and I kissed her again, knowing I could do a better job than her earlier boyfriend. I could tell I did.

But the kissing didn't last long. A campus policeman tapped on my Volkswagen's window, then pointed to his watch, indicating that Marianne was breaking curfew. I walked her to the door, kissed her again, and she was gone.

I watched from my car as her room light came on, and I watched until it went off, and I sat and stared at the dark window. I stared too long. The policeman tapped on my window again. I unrolled it. "Son, I know you are in love, but it is time to go," he said with the wisdom of an older man who had watched the ways of the young for years. I drove back to Foster's Store. . . .

19

The moon and the stars and the planets must have aligned as they should for my happiness. Those were the carefree days. That time was a warm spring, or if you wish, a crisp fall day for me. Winter's harshness and summer's heat had disappeared in my life. I had Marianne. My grades were good. I had friends, my little car, and a shabby but pleasant place to live. In my life, I have owned more stuff, but none of it made me happier than I was in those days.

Marianne and I were always together as if we were married, but not quite. Today we would move in together, but our culture did not accept that then, and this lack of complete familiarity produced a respect in me for Marianne that otherwise might not have existed. She remained mysterious. All of her, the mystery of her, her goodness, her scent, her beauty, her humor, and her charm, consumed me. I ached to make love to her but did not want to push her. I knew she hungered for me. Sometimes things just happen:

That night I had tried my shot at gourmet cooking. In time, I became better at it, but such as it was, we enjoyed the meal. We shared a bottle of Merlot while we listened to the Crosby, Stills, and Nash album. I played the song "Sweet Judy Blue Eyes" over and over. I couldn't get enough of it.

"Good Lord, Rick, you are going to wear that song out," Marianne said. "Let the album play through this time." When the song finished, I did not pick up the needle and play it again. With my glass of wine, I sat beside her on our shabby couch and, of course, we kissed, but this time it went deeper. Perhaps the wine, or the music, or perhaps it was just time.

"I want you," I said. I began touching her breast under her bra. Her nipple rose between my fingers.

"I want you, too," she said.

"You sure?"

"Yes."

"Let's go to the bedroom."

"Okay," she softly said in her southern accent. I knew it was her first time. We walked to my little bedroom and in my bed, we lay together undressing and embracing each other. I had dreamed of having her, and my dream became a reality. I saw her body for the first time. Young and firm, it surpassed my expectations. I stayed calm. It felt as if we were always lovers, as if this was not our first time together, and we made love with the tenderness she deserved. Afterward, we lay in my bed.

She snuggled to me then said, "Well, I'm not a virgin anymore. They say the first time is awful. I thought it was wonderful."

"I guess I will have to marry you then," I said it and I meant it, but I had no intention of saying such a thing then.

"I guess you will, but you aren't getting out that light. If you want me, you gotta do it right."

"What do you mean?"

"I want a real proposal and a big, fat ring and a big fat wedding," she said.

"Spoken like a true southern belle," I said.

"Rick."

"What?"

"I love you."

"I love you, too, Marianne, and I always will. With me it was love at first sight."

She rolled away and pushed up on her hands. Her perfectly proportioned breast swayed beneath her. She laughed then said, "Under the circumstances, baby, I can't say it was love at first sight with me." Then she kissed me on the neck.   I laughed and pulled her to me. Again, I felt her breast's warmth and her scent calmed me. By now the stereo played Crosby, Stills, and Nash's song "Wooden Ships." I knew every word of "Judy Blue Eyes" but never noticed the frightening lyrics to this song."

I can see by your coat, my friend you're from the
other side. There's just one thing I got to know.
Can you tell me please . . . who won?

I drifted away in thought for a moment and a sliver of fear shot through me. I stared at the ceiling. Marianne rolled away, pushed to her hands again, then looked directly into my eyes, "What's wrong?" she said.

"Nothing, that song is depressing, what with the war and everything. That's all."

Today when I hear the Crosby, Stills and Nash album, the memories of that day with

Marianne come to me like the smell of grandma baking cookies. It was the best day of my life.

A popular song's lyrics from that day were borrowed from Ecclesiastes chapter three, "To every time there is a season." Young adulthood is the season of the matchmaker with all the happiness, unhappiness, euphoria, and disappointment that occur in the paring process.

When I returned to Foster's Store from class one day, Nancy Garner sat on our couch. I had known her since we were toddlers, but I did not know her as well as I did Connie. We entered school and graduated together and I took her to the seventh-grade dance.

Travis had a crush on her since he first saw her early in our freshman year. He told me she was the most beautiful girl he had ever seen. "She is good looking, but I wouldn't go that far," I said. Travis asked her for dates several times, but she had refused until now.

Nancy sat on the couch in the living room alone. She wore a ladylike small flower print dress in tan and brown tones which went will with her brown hair that curled to her shoulders.

"Whoa, what are you doing here?" I asked in surprise as I stumbled in with an arm load of books I had gotten from the library.

"Travis invited me."

"Where is he?"

"In the kitchen," she said. Travis walked down the hall.

"Don't go out with him, Nancy. He has VD."

"I told you I would get a date with her," Travis said as he entered the living room.

I looked at Nancy, "What'd he do? Sing like Elvis for you."

"No, not yet."

"He will sooner or later," I said as I walked to my bedroom.

"Will you?"

Travis began singing "Loving You." I could feel Nancy swoon all the way to my room as I sat at my desk trying to read.

"God, you're disgusting, Travis," I yelled, but in truth, I was glad he was seeing her. Nancy and Marianne were friends.

Jake was the only one of the store-mates who did not have a girlfriend. He made some new friends, though, all male and all with long hair. Tony's girlfriend lived in Atlanta.

One afternoon, someone knocked on my door. To my surprise, a high school classmate stood there.

"Monty, what are you doing here?"

"I transferred from Georgia State. I'm on the golf team." I knew Monty was a prodigy on the golf course and in the pool hall, so I wasn't surprised.

"Is Jake here?" he asked.

"Not right now."

His hair was blond and bushy. He wore an orange and yellow Hawaiian style shirt, white Bermuda shorts, and flip-flops as if he were at the beach, and I suppose at the beach is the best way to describe him. Always carefree, he was the most charismatic person I had ever known.

I invited him in and we talked for about a half-hour. Jake did not come home while Monty and I talked, but eventually they found each other, and from that day, Monty became a big part of Jake's life, and mine. Monty charmed his way on to the golf course at the country club where he hustled the wealthy. He could win your money, and make you like it.

For the rest of 1968 and in to 1969, things at Foster's Store stayed the same, me with Marianne, Travis with Nancy, and Jake hanging out with Monty and the guys. They were good days. . . .

20

I have heard it said that auto racing began when someone built the second car. Racing is hardwired into our brains. Human beings race everything, each other, horses, dogs, turtles, and time. The day we moved into Foster's Store and Tony came in his new GTO and Travis in his, I knew there was soon to be a race.

Nineteen-sixty-eight was in the muscle car era, a time when the big three American car manufactures battled each other to put the fastest car on the road. General Motors entered the Pontiac GTO into the brawl, much to the enthusiasm of many young men.

Ronnie and the Daytonas captured their feelings about the car when they sang, "Little GTO, You're really looking fine."

The leaves were turning, but the temperature was mild, a Saturday in the fall. Tony, Travis, Jake, Monty, and I sat outside in front of the store on chairs taken from our dining table. Marianne and Nancy were at their dorm. I was trying to be Bob Dylan, playing "Girl from the North Country" on my guitar. I sang along with my strumming which was something I normally did not do. My song prompted Jake and Travis to tell both often heard bad singing jokes: What did you do with the money your mother gave you for singing lessons, and can you sing *Far, Far Away*. I chose not to sing at all after they teased me but continued to strum.

Travis chewed on a big wad of Bazooka bubble gum. His jaw was moving up and down when Tony said, "My car is faster than yours."

Travis stopped chewing, looked at Tony, then said, "No fucking way," the correct Georgia redneck response to such a challenge. He blew a bubble. It popped.

"Oh, yeah," said Tony

"Oh, yeah."

"Well, we'll see about that."

"Well, okay."

The race was to be a friendly affair. They planned to do it down the road in a flat spot where highway 166 crosses the Little Tallapoosa River. Just the two went, but they were not alone.

I do not know whether the man who watched them was the County Sheriff or a high-ranking deputy. He was six-two and two-hundred and fifty pounds, in his mid-forties, maybe fifties, with salt and pepper hair. He sat on his front porch watching as Tony and Travis turned around in his driveway. They did not see the patrol car parked beside his house. They did not see him walk to it.

From behind the steering wheel, Tony counted off the race, "Ready, set, go." Both engines roared, and the big sheriff put on his hat. The racing cars were evenly matched. Luck would decide the winner. Sometimes Tony was ahead by an inch or two, sometimes Travis. When they saw the sheriff's blue lights in their rearview mirrors, Tony let Travis pass.

I was still sitting outside. Jake and Monty had gone back inside. With no one around, I was singing again, "If you are traveling in the North Country fair, where the wind blows heavy on the border line," when Travis roared by going over a hundred miles per hour. My singing stopped, and my mouth fell open. Then Tony turned into the parking lot at sixty. He did a fishtail and the car came to rest under the canopy facing the direction from which it came. I didn't know whether Tony meant to do that or was just plain lucky. He ran inside, hoping the sheriff would pass by without stopping. I could imagine him saying, "Officer it must have been another white GTO. I've been here watching cartoons all morning," but that didn't happen.

The big sheriff got out of his car. He walked to me. His chest puffed. His cheeks turned red. "Son," he said, "where is the guy that was driving that car, and don't even think about telling me you don't know."

I whined, "I think he's inside, Sir."

"What do you mean, you *think* he's inside. YOU KNOW DAMN GOOD AND WELL HE IS IN THERE."

"Yes, Sir," I squeaked.

The sheriff started to the door, but before he got to it, Tony came out. Travis returned. He turned into the store's parking lot as if he had stepped out to buy a pack of cigarettes. No doubt, he intended to tell the big sheriff, "It was another blue GTO. I was at the convenience store in town," but one look at the sheriff told him he would never get away with it. He marched to the big sheriff with head high and shoulders back as if he had nothing to hide, then said, "Officer, what seems to be the problem here."

The big sheriff's face grew redder and his chest puffed further. He looked at Travis. He slowly let out a breath, "Boy," he said in a low growling voice. He took another breath and his face grew even redder. "Boy," he paused. "YOU KNOW DAMN GOOD AND WELL WHAT THE PROBLEM IS!" Then he yelled even louder, "YOU KNOW WHAT THE PROBLEM IS. NOW DON'T YOU!" His face became cherry red.

"Yes, Sir," Travis squealed.

Sometimes parents are proud of their offspring. *Sometimes* they win the spelling bee. *Sometimes* they hit a home run, but sometimes they don't.

I don't think either Travis's or Tony's parents were having a good moment when they brought their sons back to Foster's Store that night, after getting them out of the Carroll County jail. "Yeah, Yeah, my little *GTO. . . ."*

21

I picked up Marianne at her dorm. "Mom called," I said as she got in the car. "My draft notice came. I have to report to the draft board for my physical on March 16."

Marianne's face drew tight with lips turned down and her eyes moistened. "Oh, no, Rick, are you drafted?"

"No, not yet. It's just a physical, but they're getting closer. As long as I don't flunk out of school, I'm okay." She drew close to me and kissed my cheek. "They can't take my baby away from me."

"Oh, yes, the hell they can. They took my father from my mother in World War II," I said.

Marianne stared ahead, "One of my high school friends got shot over there."

"One of mine got killed, and a couple are in the hospital recovering from their wounds. One will never walk again."

Every young man in Atlanta knew where to report for his draft physical. The building was infamous. It sat down the street from the big Sears store on Ponce de Leon, across and down the street from where the old Atlanta Crackers baseball team played before the Braves moved to town. The Ford Motor Company built the building to house a Model T factory, but I would have never guessed that. From the front, it looked like an office building, four stories tall and made of red brick. Today, the building houses luxury condominiums.

As I walked to the door, someone called to me. I turned to see Billy West, a high school friend. He looked the same, except the length of his hair.

"What are you doing here?" I asked before I realized the question was ridiculous.

"Oh, I don't know. I felt like taking a tour of an old Model T factory," he said.

I laughed. "Yeah, me too."

"Did you see the war protest here on the news the other day?"

"Billy, there are so many war protests in the news these days; I don't guess I realized it happened here," I said.

"Well, it happened here. They gave the guys getting drafted hell, yelling and throwing stuff at them. I joined the antiwar movement back at UNC. I've been to three antiwar demonstrations, one in Washington. It was fun, man, lots of pot and lots of girls, willing girls, if you know what I mean."

"You were in Washington?"

"Yeah, but I'm not going back to school. I flunked out, too much partying."

"Jesus, Billy, if you aren't in school your ass is grass."

"Tell me about it. . . . You still got your student deferment?" Billy asked.

"Yeah."

"Well, don't fuck it up."

We walked inside. A soldier directed us to a room. It looked like a classroom with rows of school desks and on each desk sat a stack of paperwork. We filled it out. Then a soldier in starched fatigues and spit-shined boots led us into a large room. He lined us up in formation. We waited. A black man in a white hospital coat marched into the room, also wearing spit-shined boots. He spoke with authority, as if he had done his job many times before, and with good humor hidden in his voice.

"Gentlemen," he said, "welcome to the Atlanta Induction Center. I am Sergeant Barnes of the United States Army. You are here to take a physical to see whether you are fit enough to be drafted into the United States Army. It's a great honor to be selected to serve. I repeat. It is a great honor to be selected to serve." No one challenged his statement. With so much resistance against the draft, it surprised me.

"If you cooperate, we will have you out of here in a couple of hours. If not, it can take all day. That's up to you. I have all the time in the world. My enlistment is up in three years. The room behind me is a locker room, and there you will disrobe. Put your belongings into a locker. Bring the key with you. It is attached to an elastic cord, so you can wear it around your neck." He held up a key with the cord attached. After you undress, return here and line up exactly as you are now." We undressed and returned to our formation.

"Gentlemen, I, Sergeant Nathaniel Barnes of the United States Army, have the worst job in the entire United States Army as you shall shortly see. It is time to check you for rupture," he said as he put on rubber gloves. "I will walk up to you and stick my finger deep into your scrotum. You turn your head to the right and cough. I do not like doing this anymore than you like having it done; however, if you do like me touching you, I have some extra paperwork for you to fill out. The United States Army does not accept homosexuals, so if you are homosexual speak up now." No one did. It was an easy way out of the draft, but no one wanted the stigma, even the homosexuals.

When he finished, he said, "Gentlemen that is not the worst part of my job. No, no, the worst is yet to come. Now, you may be asking yourself what could be worse than that. . . . Well, this is. It's time to check for hemorrhoids. By the time we finish, I will know your asshole intimately. Bend over and spread your cheeks. Again, I don't like doing this anymore than you like having it done."

He examined each of us. When finished he said, "Gentlemen, you may return to the locker room and dress. Even though you think you are the sexiest man alive, let me assure you that you are not, and the nurses and secretaries here do not wish to see any part of you in the nude. The physical is not over. After you are dressed, return to this room. From here you will follow the yellow tiles in the floor to the next station. Got it? Follow the yellow brick road like in the *Wizard of Oz*. You can do that, can't you?"

About half the men carried their medical records, which chronicled their sicknesses or injuries. For the first time, asthma sufferers were glad they had asthma, and flat feet were a blessing.

"Look at these liars," Billy said. "I wonder how many took Benzedrine to raise their blood pressure."

"You don't have to do that. Did you know that if you hold a bar of Octagon soap under your arm, it will raise your blood pressure sky-high?"

"Yeah, I heard that. I thought about becoming a conscientious objector. I don't want to kill anybody."

"Me, either" I said.

"But they won't give me conscientious objector status, without a big court fight. I thought about becoming a Quaker. Anybody who grew up as a Quaker or Mennonite can get conscientious objector status easily, but they won't buy it if your religious epiphany occurs a week before you get drafted."

"If they did, the Quakers would become the biggest church in the country."

"You know what, man? They leave me no choice. I'm going to Canada. They can't get me there."

"You're kidding, right? Billy you're kidding?"

"No, the hell I'm not." He finished dressing and walked to the door. "Tell Sergeant Barnes goodbye for me." I never saw Billy again.

22

No one else at Foster's Store received a draft physical notice. The Draft Board renewed my student deferment, so my draft status stayed the same through my junior and into my senior years. During the summer breaks, the Foster's Store crew went home. Travis, Nancy, Marianne, and I often double dated in Atlanta. Travis and I stayed at my parent's. Marianne spent the weekends close by at Nancy's parent's house.

Nancy's parent's home had a large family room. It was downstairs, separate from the rest of the house. When we had nothing else to do, we congregated there with friends from the neighborhood or college. Sometimes Jake was there, and sometimes he spent his time with Monty and his new friends. Nancy's parents, more liberal than mine, didn't mind if we drank beer there assuming we drank it responsibly which we did. We were almost the legal drinking age anyway.

Nancy forbid us to watch the news. "It's too depressing," she said, but we did watch the coverage of the music festival at Woodstock.

"Good God, look at that," I said as the camera panned the crowd.

The TV announcer said that more than four-hundred-thousand youths crowded into a farmer's field in Woodstock, New York to hear the most popular rock bands. He listed the crowd's favorites: Crosby, Stills, Nash and Young; Jimi Hendrix, Arlo Guthrie, Joan Baez, Credence Clearwater Revival, Can Heat, Jefferson Airplane, and country Joe and the Fish. The coverage showed the crowd singing along with Country Joe's Vietnam War protest song:

"And it's one, two, three, what're we fighting for?
Don't ask me, I don't give a damn
Next stop is Vietnam."

At Atlanta's Fox Theater, we watched Peter Fonda's classic movie *Easy Rider*. Travis didn't like it. In the movie, Peter Fonda is a biker who gets killed by a Louisiana redneck. "That coin flips both ways," Travis said. "My senior year of high school a group of bikers beat the shit out of me."

"What'd you do to piss them off?" I asked.

"It happened here in Atlanta. A friend and I came down from Cartersville. We were lost. Traffic stopped right in front of this biker bar. They were drunk and all out in the street. One jumped on the hood of my car. Traffic kept us from moving. I made the mistake of getting out, and my buddy got out to help me and they beat the shit out of us."

The rest of us didn't agree with Travis. We thought it was a good movie and I still do.

During those two summers, I grew to know Marianne's family. I had no idea, nor did Marianne, that her mother worked against me.

I love southern women. Most are what they seem to be, genuinely nice, but that charm is the perfect camouflage for the scheming to do their dirty work, and some southern women will politely put a knife between your ribs and smile while they do it, and smile while they claim they knew nothing about it, and if she has done her job well, you will think she is either too sweet or stupid to have done such a lowdown thing. They make excellent lawyers.

Yankee women are no match. Marianne's mother could do this if needed to get her way.

She was the daughter of an Alabama farmer, great-granddaughter of a plantation owner. Her family acted as if they had money, though they did not. She earned a degree in Education at Troy State University in Alabama, but she never taught. Instead, she got a job as a flight attendant with a fledgling little airline named Delta. In the 1940s, a flight attendant job was a breakthrough job for women. She refused to accept the traditional woman's roles as a schoolteacher, nurse, or secretary.

Marianne's father survived twenty-one missions over Europe in World War II as a B17 pilot. When the war ended, he took a job at Delta where he met Marianne's mother. They married. A year later, Marianne was born. I liked her father. I liked him a lot.

My father had a copy of *Life's Picture History of World War II,* and from the time I was five, I studied it. The pictures made a mark on me; more than that, they haunted me. I understood more than most what he had experienced in the war, and I respected him for it. Marianne's father was a warm, gracious, and a genuinely good person. Surviving the war made him a religious man. He was a Methodist.

Marianne's mother encouraged Marianne to date her earlier boyfriend, the one who wore letter sweaters. His name was Norman, and Norman's father was old Atlanta money, a lawyer for the law firm whose main account was the Coca-Cola Company. She thought her family deprived of her rightful social standing, and she saw Norman as a chance to restore the correct order of things. Though, my father was a successful businessman, she saw him as a shopkeeper and me as a shopkeeper's son. I know now, she just didn't like me, though she never said this to Marianne or me. At the least, she wanted Marianne to marry a pilot like her father. She schemed to make it happen.

23

The next fall back at Foster's Store, I washed dishes in the kitchen. Marianne watched TV in the living room. She called, "Rick, come here quick."

I ran to the living room in time to see Monty in handcuffs on TV. The camera focused on an open briefcase full of hundred-dollar bills. Then it showed the others who were arrested. I watched in disbelief.

"Marianne, I know every one of those guys. They're all from my neighborhood. One is a politician's son."

Monty and the others had filled a DC4 cargo plane with marijuana. I assume it came from Central America. With a bulldozer, they graded a runway on a mountain top in Polk County where the plane landed, but the runway wasn't long enough for it to take off. Locals saw the plane come down and assumed it crashed. They called the police. Monty and the others were arrested. The TV newsman reported that Monty said, "What money?" when asked about the suitcase full of one-hundred-dollar bills. That sounds like him, I thought.

"Where's Jake?" Marianne asked.

"I don't know. I haven't seen him all day."

"You don't suppose. . ."

"Oh, God, I hope not."

"Let's go look for him."

Marianne and I drove around campus and talked with his friends. No one had seen him all day. We returned to Foster's Store.

An hour later, he came in. "Where have you been? We've been worried to death," Marianne said as if she had given birth to him.

"I met a girl. Her name is Alice. She's really neat."

Jake knew nothing about Monty's pot smuggling venture. "It hurts me that you think I would get involved in something like that."

"Well, you and Monty were pretty tight."

"I know, and I knew he sold a little pot, but I didn't know anything about this."

It was the largest marijuana bust in history, though larger ones have been made since. Someone made a movie about it called *In Hot Pursuit (The Polk County Pot Plane)*. The plane sat on the mountain for years before someone extended the runway and flew it off.

"Tell me about this girl you met," I said.

"Her name is Alice Graham and she's really neat," Jake said again. "She is an activist for the National Organization of Women. You know about them?"

"Yeah, I saw them on the news. They want equal pay for equal work. I don't have a problem with that. It's only fair, and they burned their bras. Come to think about it, I don't have a problem with that either."

I expected Alice to look like the feminists I had seen on TV, angry, braless, style-less, hippie women, but that was not Alice. Her dress had a hippie flare, but still stylish. Anger was not in her nature. Kindness was. I thought Jake had done well for himself. Alice's hair was blond. Her shapely frame stood only five-three. She and Jake hung out with Marianne, Nancy, Travis, and me, but still spent much time away with her friends and Jake's new friends. Alice supported legalized abortion. She told Marianne and me why.

"Before I came here, I attended a little Christian college on Atlanta's east side. I got pregnant. Not only did I get pregnant, I got pregnant by one of the instructors, a married man. I wanted to go to one of those homes for pregnant teen girls, but he knew a better way, or so he said."

In those days, most parents managed unwanted teenage pregnancy by sending the pregnant teen to a home for unwed mothers. The teen told her friends that she needed to visit a sick aunt for a while, and everybody believed her, or at least pretended to. She gave birth then put the baby up for adoption. Normally, she had no trouble finding a home for the baby.

Alice continued. "He took me to a motel on Highway 41, in Marietta. I thought the abortionist would be a man. A woman showed up. She used a turkey baster with the front cut to make the hole larger. Can you believe it, a frickin turkey baster? I had always heard they used coat hanger wire. She squirted the fetus into the toilet and I saw it. It looked like a small baby. I threw up. No girl should go through that. I could have died from infection. I bled for several days, but it finally stopped. When I heard about the National Organization of Women, I joined it."

When I was eleven, I rode the bus to downtown Atlanta, headed to Rich's, Atlanta's leading department store. The city was safe enough for a child to ride the bus into the city in those days. My Dad's tux shop sat close to Rich's, and I planned to ride home with him.

The normally busy downtown streets were empty, except a crowd of protesters in front of Rich's. They marched in a circle at the main entrance and the Ku Klux Klan marched around them, but I knew nothing about the Klan and wondered why they were dressed in silly white sheets like children at Halloween. A black man in a blue business suit was making a speech. The TV news cameras were there. I didn't know what was happening, and I didn't care. I was on a mission. I had discovered rock and roll and wanted a Jerry Lee Lewis record.

I avoided the crowd by using a side entrance. There were no other customers in the store. I bought the records and walked back to my Dad's store.

"What's going on at Rich's?" I asked my father and described the scene to him.

"What!" he said. "I'll be right back." He walked out, leaving my Grandfather and me behind. In a few minutes, he returned.

"It's Martin King's boy again, isn't it?" my Grandfather said. He always called Martin Luther King Jr. Martin's boy because he knew his father, but that was not unusual. Martin Luther King Sr. knew many Atlantans, and so did my grandfather.

"Yes," my father said. "They're trying to integrate the lunch counter at Rich's. The Klan is there," he said. Then he looked at me, "Son, don't go down there again. There could be big trouble. . . ."

I was driving to Carrollton. My memories of Martin Luther King roared through my mind as the car radio blurted, "Martin Luther King Jr. has been killed in Memphis."

I ran off the road. Oh, shit! I regained control of my VW. *Who would want to do something like that?* Then I thought better, *plenty of people would.*

I pulled into a country store to buy a drink. One of the customers asked the clerk, "Did you hear? Somebody killed the fucking nigger Martin Luther King."

"Good riddance," the clerk said.

Good riddance! . . . Is that what I am? Is that man me? He's a southerner. I'm a southerner. King changed America for the better, and they killed him for doing it. They killed King for changing me. They killed King for changing everything. . . . Confusion came, and shame. Only a few years ago, John Kennedy was assassinated. In a few months, Robert Kennedy would also be assassinated. Uncertainty and fear gripped the country. That night, people rioted. City after city burned. America bled and it showed in the nightly news, night after night, after night:

"Today, in some of the heaviest fighting ever in Vietnam, one hundred and fifty US soldiers died in what is now being called the Tet offensive. . . ."

"Today, in Detroit, riots continued. Large sections of that city are in flames. . . ."

"Today, in the recapture of Hue, Vietnam, eighty-three American soldiers were killed. . . ."

"Today, at Harvard, war protesting students burned the ROTC building. . ."

"Today, in Saigon, heavy fighting was reported at the American Embassy. We are told hundreds have been killed and the embassy has been overrun. . ."

At the Democrat National Convention, antiwar demonstrators chanted, "The whole world is watching. The whole world is watching. The whole world is watching," as the police beat them with billy clubs. Their chant haunted me. *The whole world is watching.*

But one news story was hopeful. "Marianne, did you hear that? They're going to do a draft lottery by birthday."

"What do you mean?"

"They're going to put every day of the year in a bowl and pull them out. The men born on the first day they pull from the bowl will be the first drafted. The men born on the second birthday pulled will be the second group drafted, and so forth until they get all they need. The birthdays pulled after the 195th day will not serve. The lottery will be on TV. Maybe I'll get lucky. . . ."

24

We thought about having a draft lottery party, but decided the occasion was much too somber for that. The night of the lottery, Marianne and I, Travis and Nancy, and Jake and Alice watch the draft lottery on TV. Tony drove to Atlanta to watch with his girlfriend there.

It was my senior year, and there was no doubt the war would not end before I graduated. The country's initial patriotic spirit had vanished as the body count rose. America decided Vietnam was not worth the cost in life and treasure. America wanted out. Many thought the draft unfairly targeted the poor and minorities.

The astute, lucky or politically connected hid from Vietnam service in the National Guard.

College enrollment swelled with those more interested in escaping the draft than getting an education. Congress decided a birthday lottery was fairer. At least one could tell whether he was to be drafted. Those fortunate enough to escape it could continue their lives. The lottery did not change the college deferment. College men were drafted when they graduated, ensuring a supply of officer candidates.

We bought a case of beer. Jake brought a little pot. Every young person in America watched that night. For an unfortunate few, the lottery was the first in a series of events that led to their death. I felt as if I were a young Aztec warrior awaiting the temple priest to decide which man's heart was to be ripped out for their god Tlaxcala. But this modern Aztec priest wore no beads, no feathers. He would have been more interesting dressed that way. He was the dullest of the dull, an old, graying white man in a business suit, the uniform of power, power over me. He called the first number.

"September 14."

Travis stood by the television, "That anybody's birthday?" It wasn't.

"December 6," and so forth until the fifteenth number. "May 16," my birthday.

I knew it. I am chosen. I have always known I would have to fight. The path is set. I cannot escape. I have to do this for me, not Uncle Sam, but for me. I must face this monster. I cannot run. I would hate myself if I did.

Marianne cried. She looked up at me with wet eyes. "Let's get married, Rick, let's do it before you go."

My mouth formed a word and said it as if my mind were not in control, "No." *It's too much. I can't do both at the same time. I cannot do this married.* My stomach twisted, my face tensed. I was angry. Marianne still cried.

The lottery continued one number after the other in rapid succession, "June 6, August 8, October 4," and then, "February 16."

Jake jumped up. "Goddamn, son of a bitch." He lit a cigarette. He slammed the door as he went outside. Alice followed.

"Don't do it, Jake. Fight it. Don't do it," she said.

"Don't worry, baby, I'm gonna fight it. I ain't going. Fuck the son of a bitches. I don't believe in war. I'll go to Canada before I'll go to Vietnam."

I walked outside.

"You gonna do it?" he asked.

"I have to," I said.

"Why?"

"I just have to. That's all."

"You're fucking crazy," he said.

Jake and I were against the war. We saw it exactly the same; but I chose to face it directly. He chose to escape it. In either choice, there was a price to pay. Things were never the same between Jake and me after that moment, but I still loved him and always will.

They drew Travis's birthday near the end. He escaped. Somehow, I knew he would. He was always lucky. Some are destined to walk an easy path. Some are not.

I must do this, and I must do it alone. I became an ass-hole. There is no other way to put it. I could not do this in love. I could not care too much whether I lived or died. I prepared myself. I girded for the fight. Light and quick, I needed no baggage. I needed no love. I distanced myself from my friends. I became angry, and I pushed Marianne away. She didn't understand what was happening. The closer to graduation, the worse I became. Finally, I made her cry. I made her cry.

"Rick, what's wrong?" she asked. I sat on the sofa watching TV.

"Nothing."

"You haven't said two words to me all day."

"Really."

"Talk to me."

"Hush, I am watching *Laugh-In*."

"Rick."

"WHAT," I yelled at her for the first time.

"I don't understand, honey, what's wrong."

"Nothing, just leave me the fuck alone."

"I'm going back to the dorm." Tears were in her eyes.

"Good!" I drove her back to her dorm. On the way, we did not say a word to each other and she sobbed. I did not kiss her goodnight, and I never called her again. I did that. I did that. I never called. I ended it. I set my jaw. I could not allow love to weaken me. It was over.

Our senior year was ending. It ended for all but me. I fell behind because of the fiasco with English 101. I enrolled in summer school, but I did not live in Carrollton. I drove from Atlanta three days a week to take one class. I finished, but there was no graduation ceremony until the next May. By then I would be in the Army.

I had it the way it had to be for me. I stepped into life's next stage alone. I walked alone and that is the way I wanted it. At first I did not look back.

25

The snow fell. It clung to my shoulders and wet my cheeks. The wind roared in my ears. The Draft Board told us to bring as little as possible. The Army would provide everything we needed. They also told us we were going by bus to Fort Jackson, South Carolina where the climate is the same as Atlanta's, but we flew to Fort Knox, Kentucky. My dress was for Fort Jackson. I wore only a Pendleton shirt for a jacket. Most of us made the same mistake. We stood in the snow at parade rest, waiting for the drill sergeant to return.

Until that morning, I had never heard of parade rest. The drill sergeant taught us how to do it. He told us not to move, then left us about midnight.

The sun peeked over the horizon and we were still there.

The drill sergeant finally returned. He marched us to a barracks, the wooden two-story type built for World War II. I noticed red coffee cans nailed to the wooden support posts. "Butts" was written on them, just as I had seen in the movies. Oddly, it made me feel connected to the men of World War II and I liked that. We stripped to our underwear and got into the beds.

At last some sleep, but it didn't last long. Someone beat on a large mess hall pan with a serving spoon, *clang, clang, clang.*

"Good morning, ladies," the drill sergeant yelled. "Welcome to the United States Army. Your heart may belong to your mama, but your ass belongs to me. Get up. We're going to chow. We've got a full day ahead." *Oh, God* I thought. I stumbled out of bed, dressed, and marched to the chow hall with the others. I had my first taste of Army chow that morning, and it was okay.

A half-hour later, we stood at attention by our bunks. The drill sergeant poked *in* our stomachs and *out* our chests. "Hold that head up, soldier," the drill sergeant yelled directly into a man's face. The man did as he said, even so the drill sergeant yelled. "I have never seen a more pathetic group of ladies in my life."

"Yes, sir," the man said.

"What did you call me!"

"Sir, sir."

"Sir, I work for a living. I'm an enlisted man. You call officers sir. You call me drill sergeant. Got it!"

"Yes, sir."

"What! What did you just say?"

"I mean yes drill sergeant, sir."

"What!"

"I mean, yes, drill sergeant."

"That's better."

He marched us to the barbershop. "Take a little off the top and trim up the sides," one of the recruits said. The barber did not smile. Everyone made the same joke. *Buzz, buzz.* The trainee's carefully groomed Elvis locks hit the floor. "That will be fifty-cents," the barber said. You had to pay for the haircut no one wanted. Next came the inoculations.

"Step up on the platform. After you get inoculated, step off the platform so the next man can step up." Medics with pneumatic jet syringes stood on each side of the platform. I stepped up. I felt the sting of the injection.

"Hey, hey, man, move!" I could not get off the platform. *Shit,* I felt the sting again. I told a medic. He looked concerned but said, "Don't worry about it." I forgot it, and went on.

We spent the rest of the day getting our boots, uniforms, helmets, and such. The gear smelled of new dye and fresh leather. That night the barracks filled with the smell of shoe polish as we spit shined our boots.

In only a few weeks, I could shoot straight, throw a grenade, fire a M60 machine gun, fire a fifty-cal, set up a Claymore, fire a M72 LAW, gouge your eyes out, and kick you in the balls. I ran fast. I ran long. I swung from bar to bar like a monkey, I pushed up. I sat up, marched and sang cadences as our running boots tromped simultaneously on the pavement and our unit standard flew before us.

"I wanna be an Airborne Ranger.
I wanna live a life of danger.
I wanna go to Vietnam. Hooah."

We sang it often, but it puzzled me. We weren't Airborne Ranges, but we were becoming a tight group, and I liked it.

Sometimes Hollywood gets it right. The movie stereotypes were all there, the guy from

155

Brooklyn, an intellectual, the comedian, the guy who "just couldn't take it anymore," and, of course, the platoon screw-up who dropped a grenade with the pin pulled. Our Drill Sergeant tackled him and dove with him behind a wall, thus saving the platoon screw-up from becoming the ex-platoon screw-up.

The mail came daily and daily some soldier's eyes grew soft with moisture; though, in front of his buddies, he would never let the moisture grow into tears.

"She said she would love me forever."

"What's the matter? Jody gets your girl?" He received little sympathy.

"Welcome to the real world," a trainee who had already received a "Dear John" letter said to the hurting man.

Jody was an imaginary man who stole your girlfriend while you were away. Jody and his friends lured away all but a few. World War II era women waited for their men. Vietnam era women did not. I didn't know why. But I did know I would not receive a Dear John letter. I was smart. I had protected myself. I had broken up with Marianne, but at night I could not get her out of my dreams.

One day everything became harder to do than usual. I fell behind. Next morning at breakfast, the man who sat across from me said, "What the hell are all those red blotches on your face. You'd better go on sick call."

I did, and they put me in the hospital. I had the measles. Perhaps the double injections caused it. I don't know. I slept for five days. After a few days, my drill sergeant began trying to get my release. We had a common interest. He did not want to recycle me, and I did not want to be recycled. They kept me in the hospital as long as possible without recycling me, then released me probably early, but I didn't care. Next day was the physical fitness test. I had to pass it to graduate, but when I told my legs to run, they would not. When I told my arms to pull me up, they could not. I failed the test. I would be recycled.

The drill sergeant called me to his office. "Rinehart, I know damn good and well you can pass that test. Usually, command will not let you take it twice, but I am going to do my best to get permission to let you take it again."

"Yes, Drill Sergeant."

I heard no more about the retest. They scheduled the graduation ceremony for the next afternoon at the parade field.

That morning the drill sergeant called me to his office. "Go to the athletic field. See Sergeant Bender. He will retest you. When you pass, get into your dress uniform and go directly to the parade field."

This time, when I told my legs to run, they did, and when I told my arms to pull me up, they did. I caught my platoon before they entered the parade field, and when I joined them, my friends cheered for me, and it felt good. I knew I had accomplished something worth doing. The Army had made me a better man.

26

After basic training, the Army sent me to Fort Polk, Louisiana for Advanced Infantry Training. They offered me the chance to go to Officer's Candidate School. I refused it.

"Sir," I said to the recruiter, "I am a citizen soldier. I will put myself in harm's way for my country, but I cannot lead men into a conflict unless I fully believe my sacrifice and theirs is worth it. Early in this war I would say yes. If it were World War II, I would say yes, but I will not lead men into this mess. I am not your man. I would be miserable if I tried. I just can't do it."

The recruiters heard similar things from the others. The Army asked all the college graduates in my basic training Company to go to the Officer Candidate School; none did it, and perhaps in retaliation, all the college graduates were given a combat Military Occupational Specialty which put all the college men in combat units. The media told us only the poor and uneducated served in combat. In my experience, that was not so.

Eight men from my basic training platoon accompanied me to Fort Polk. A friend named Carter was one, and three of the others who came with me were National Guardsmen from the Cleveland, Ohio area. No doubt they were well-connected. Slots in the National Gard were impossible to get. I had gotten to know Bailey, one of the Guardsmen. I overlooked the fact he would not tell me how he got into the Guard. Some in my basic training company didn't. They resented him and the other guardsmen; even so, given the chance, they would have done exactly as he did.

Bailey was a quality guy, perhaps even upper class. He had graduated from Kent State University the year before, and his girlfriend still attended school there.

In the mornings as we ate breakfast, a radio played top forty music in the background, and each hour they aired the news.

"President Nixon has sent troops from Vietnam to neighboring Cambodia to destroy Vietcong and North Vietnamese supply depots there," the newscaster said.

"Oh, shit, now we've got two wars on our hands, one in Vietnam and one in Cambodia," Baily said. Nixon planned to return the troops to Vietnam after they destroyed the supplies. Distrust of the government was high. No one believed him.

The invasion of Cambodia caused a wave of war protest on college campuses, especially at Kent State University, Bailey's alma mater. A few days later, at breakfast, the radio played as usual.

"And now the news, protesting students at Kent State University have burned the ROTC building there. Governor Rhodes has sent the National Guard to restore order."

Bailey dropped his coffee.

He found a payphone and called his girlfriend. "I'm all right," she said. "All our friends were there. The soldiers put bayonets on their guns, but they didn't stab anybody. There is another demonstration tonight."

"Be careful honey. I am proud of you. I love you. Oh, what Guard unit is there?"

"The 1st of the 145th, something like that. What's your unit?"

"The 1st of the . . . 145th," he said.

A few weeks later, Rock Star Neil Young sang:

Tin soldiers and Nixon coming,
We're finally on our own.
This summer I hear the drumming,
Four dead in Ohio.

The 1st of the 145th killed four students and injured nine, and Bailey didn't know "whether to shit or go blind."

One morning at formation, the drill sergeant came to me, "Rinehart, did you graduate from college?" he asked.

"Yes, Drill Sergeant."

"Did you go through the ceremony?"

"No, Drill Sergeant."

"Do you know when it is?"

"No, Drill Sergeant."

"Tomorrow at 2:00 and you are going to be there. Go to the orderly room."

My father arranged it, though I didn't understand how. From the orderly room, I went to the airport, and by that evening I was home enduring comments from my family about my hair, how strong I looked, and how much weight I had lost.

"Look at you. You stand so straight. You don't look like the same person," Mom said.

A Georgia spring is God's spring, a new-life, green spring to perfection, accented by the bright colored flowers brought to life by the warm Georgia sun. This day was like that. I was home. I was where I belonged. Everything was familiar, yet everything had changed.

The graduating class was the class behind mine; even so, I knew most there. I knew them but they no longer knew me. I was in the military, and I may as well have had the plague. My haircut and stature gave me away.

I saw a poster in the student center. Three attractive college girls sat in a row. The poster said, "Girls say yes to boys who say no," to the draft was implied.

At the ceremony, I sat next to Marianne's friend Beth. She said nothing.

Finally, I asked, "Beth, how are you?"

"Fine, oh, Rick, I didn't recognize you. How are you?. What happened to your hair?"

"I'm in the Army,"

"The Army, ooooh." She looked away and said no more.

Not one fucking person spoke to me that day. My father tried to do something special for me, but bigger things than family love were at work. I wanted to get out of Carrollton and back to Fort Polk where there was less pain. That weekend, my friend Carter and I got drunk on 3.2 Army beer. It took a lot. . . .

27

Fort Polk was humid, so humid that the fatigues we brought from Fort Knox became sticky as the starch in them soaked up the Louisiana moisture. We sent all our starched clothing to the laundry.

Louisiana is hot like Vietnam and it is wooded, but not as thick as the jungles are there. I felt at home at Fort Polk. This part of Louisiana wasn't much different from my part of Georgia. We continued our training. In a war game, the enemy captured me. I knew that immediately after your capture is the best time to escape, so I tried and got in a fight with a sergeant. Others came to his rescue, and when they subdued me I was bloody and he was too. It's faded now, but for a long time my arm was scarred where he hit me with his rifle, no grudge held, just part of training.

We were at Fort Polk to learn mortars. Carter, my buddy from basic training, made the trip to Louisiana with me. He grew up in Buford, Georgia. His father managed a bra factory there, an unusual job I thought. Carter joked about it. He looked like all young soldiers, same haircut, same uniform. His eyes were blue, his nose was larger than average, and he was tall, very tall.

We were on the same mortar team. I was the second gunner, the man who dropped the round down the barrel. Carter was the first gunner, the man who sighted the mortar. Others handled the ammunition and did the mathematical calculations; though, we each knew the other's jobs.

Memorial Day weekend, Carter and I got a pass. We wanted to go to New Orleans. I pictured myself on Bourbon Street with a good-looking girl under each arm. Such are the fantasies of a young man. We planned to catch the bus at Leesville, the nearest town to Fort Polk, where a section of the town exists for the sole purpose of separating money from the soldiers who carried it. The troops at Fort Polk called Leesville Sleazeville or sometimes Diseaseville.

We waited for the bus in a beer joint. A girl danced in a bird cage hung high over the beer joint's bar, but not hung so high you couldn't reach up and tip her, which Carter and I did. The more beer we drank, the more we tipped her. It seems there is a mathematical correlation between the beer and the tips, which the young woman well understood, having studied math at the local junior college where she said she was a student. She was sexy and sexy women never lie, so we helped her out as much as we could, and when we left to get on our bus, I was sure she loved me.

I have seen pictures of buses in Mexico that are so crowded that people ride on top. This bus was like that. Our laws will not allow one to ride on top, but if it did allow it, I would have. Inside the bus was steamy hot and standing room only, but several got off at our first stop, so Carter and I were able to sit. The seats were small, babies cried, people smelled, and the air conditioner did not work well.

In an hour, we stopped at Alexandria. In another hour, we arrived at our second stop, Marksville. In another hour, we arrived at our third stop, Bunkie, and after another hour, we arrived at our fourth stop, New Roads.

Then we slowed. Road construction blocked the road, but in an hour, we got under way again. In another hour, we arrived at Zachary. "Next stop Baton Rouge," the driver said.

"How many stops between Baton Rouge and New Orleans?" Carter asked.

"Three, no, four."

"Rick, we are going to spend our whole leave on this friggin' bus. I can't take it anymore; let's get off at Baton Rouge. It's a big college town we ought to be able to find something to do. LSU is there."

"I agree." *So much for Bourbon Street.* Finding a cab at the bus station wasn't a problem. "Take us to the best hotel in town," Carter said.

I cringed. The second best or third best was good enough for me and for our budget. The cab driver took us to the Roosevelt, the tallest building in Baton Rouge.

"Hey, driver, what's there to do in this town, anyway?" Carter asked. The cab driver was a long-haired man two or three years older than Carter and me.

"Well," he said, "There's the Festival of Man and Earth."

"What's that?" I asked.

"A pop festival."

"You're kidding! I said.

"Here," he handed a flier to Carter. He held it where I could see and read it aloud. "John Lee

Hooker, Chuck Berry, The Youngbloods, Brownsville Station, The Buckinghams, The Ides of March, Ted Nugent, Alice Cooper, and The Amboy Dukes. It's going on now at Thunderbird Beach."

"Good God, those are good bands. What's Thunderbird Beach like?" Carter asked.

"There's a lake. They've set up a stage like Woodstock."

Carter turned to me, "Let's go."

"Hell, yeah," I said. "But we gotta get some civilian clothes. I'm not going in my uniform."

"Good point." Carter said. "Driver, do you know where we can get some hip clothes?"

"I know just the place. I'll wait while y'all get checked in. Then I'll take you there."

"Good deal," Carter said. The cab driver's name was Bill. He took us to Koch's Department Store.

Koch was a Jew and he looked it. He wore no yarmulke but his hair was cut so that it was easily envisioned on the back of his head. The store smelled of newly dyed fabric, and it was old. Modern merchandising had not reached Koch's. His goods were neatly stacked on tables as he had done for years. My grandfather's friend, Greenberg, owned a store like this. When I was young, we went there every fall for school clothes. I felt at home in Koch's store. "May I help you?" he asked.

"We are going to that pop festival," I said.

"You mean the Festival of Man and Earth. God forbid you go in those uniforms. I can fix you right up," he said in a Yiddish accent.

Koch's personal dress was far from hip. I wasn't sure he stocked what we wanted, but I was wrong. He had everything we needed. I left wearing bell bottom jeans, black biker boots, a light-blue work shirt, and a leather vest. Carter was dressed similarly.

We got into Bill's cab. "Now the only problem is all this stuff looks new, like we bought it just to go to this festival, which we did," Carter said.

"That and our hair."

"Hey, Bill, do you know where there is a wig shop?"

"Let me think a minute," he said.

"Just kidding. If I wore a wig, it would probably fall off and land in some biker's lap," Carter said.

"Can you still tell we're in the military?" I asked Bill.

"Guys, your hair is a dead giveaway. You will be all right. You're in Baton Rouge, not Boston. LSU is here, not fucking Harvard."

"Go Dawgs," Carter said.

"Hey, we beat the shit out of you Georgia Bulldogs last year."

"Yeah, well, you got lucky,"

By now we were at Thunderbird Beach. "Park this cab and come with us," Carter said.

"Fellas, I wish I could. I'll be out there tonight, but in that crowd, I doubt I will see y'all. Have fun."

"Bill, you've been great. Thank you," I said. For low paid GIs, we tipped him well. He deserved it.

The walk from the parking lot to the show was long. The closer we came to the entrance, the thicker the crowd became. We were surrounded. A tall long-haired guy with a yellow and green headband spoke to us. "You guys escape from prison or Fort Polk."

For a second, I thought prison might be the better answer. "Fort Polk," I said. I noticed he wore an old OD green Army shirt with the name Haynes above the pocket.

"I trained there," he said.

"You go to Nam?" I asked.

"Yeah."

"How was it?"

"I'd rather not talk about it." We walked along together in silence. No one else spoke. No one else paid attention to us, and I relaxed. Then good fortune came. A group of attractive girls sat on the ground next to us, as legendary bluesman John Lee Hooker took the stage. "Boom, boom, boom, boom, I'm gonna shoot you right down," he sang.

Rick, Rick you can't let this pass. A good-looking girl is sitting two feet from you. Get over your shyness. You must speak to her. You must do it. You must speak. Do it now!

"Hello, I'm Rick."

"Hello, Rick. I'm Becky."

Whew, that wasn't so bad.

By now John Lee Hooker sang, "I'm in the mood. I'm in the moood for love," in his base delta style.

"That's where it started, the blues," I said.

"I love it. I always have," she said as she swayed her shoulders to the music. She wore a big black floppy straw hat, blue jeans shorts, and a camisole type top. Colorful flowers were painted on her sandals. Her brown hair hung to the middle of her back. She smiled.

"Me, too, I grew up listening to it," I said.

"You in the Army or something?"

"Yeah."

"Fort Polk?"

"You guessed it."

"Going to Nam?"

"Yeah."

"You afraid?"

"Naw." I lied.

"When do you leave?"

"Just a few days."

The conversation stopped. The music overcame us. I watched her, lost in its rhythm and joined her there in her ecstasy. When the music ended I ask "What do you do?

"I'm a bank teller," She said. "Did you hear the rumor? Credence Clearwater Revival might show up tonight."

"That'd be great. . . ." And the conversation grew warm, and the interest in each other became an attraction, and the day became night, and someone handed out candles, and we lit them and held them high while we sang along with the Youngbloods:

Come on people now
Smile on your brother
Everybody get together
Try to love one another
Right now.

And I kissed her in the candlelight. And I held her and trembled. And I confessed to her that I was afraid. And I stayed the night at her apartment, and we made love until the grey morning filled her window. Then she drove me to the hotel, then to the bus station, and when I walked away she cried, and I wanted to. . . .

28

After a few days at Fort Lewis, Washington and a stop in Alaska and Japan, a chartered Flying Tiger Boeing 707 flew over Cam Ranh Bay, Vietnam. We did a combat landing. It didn't feel right. I thought something was wrong.

In a combat landing, the plane descends in a circular vortex, corkscrew like-pattern. I didn't know then, but the Vietnam War was a vortex that sucked you down, and at the bottom of the vortex was the My Lai massacre.

It happened two years before I arrived. In a bloody massacre, a Lieutenant Calley's platoon killed as many as five-hundred villagers, women, children and all. Calley and his men thought the villagers supported the Viet Cong in the area who had killed several of their men. They acted on some dubious orders given by Calley's commanding officer, Captain Medina. Command covered the incident up, but there was a scandal and then a trial, Twenty-two men were charged, but they convicted only Lieutenant Calley, and he received a slap on the hand. I feel safe in saying that none of the men charged with the crimes would have ever killed anyone had they not been sucked into the Vietnam War. As I said, Vietnam was a vortex, and it sucked Calley and his men all the way to the bottom. They were both killers and casualties of the war.

I did not know it then, but Lieutenant Calley was in Charley Company of the Eleventh Brigade of the Americal Division. I was in Echo Company. Our headquarters building was next door to his. I have seen My Lai from a helicopter. The bamboo and thatch buildings were neglected, in need of repair. No one lived there, and we never went there.

The 707 landed at Cam Ranh Bay. Airmen pushed the airplane ramp to us. The door opened. I joined the line to exit. Cam Ranh Bay sits on reflective white beach sand. The light reflecting from it hit my eyes and I had to squint. The airplane ramp's handrail was too hot to touch. I didn't know what to expect. And yes, I was afraid.

We walked to a wooden pavilion with a metal roof where we filled out paperwork. A clerk took it to an office where our destiny was decided, and we went to a barracks to wait. It too was wooden with a metal roof, but like most American military buildings there, it had wooden walls about five feet high and three feet of screen above the wooden part of the wall. The Army painted the buildings OD green. They painted everything OD green, including the men. At Fort Lewis, they issued OD green jungle fatigues to us. I liked them better than the stateside fatigues.

That evening, I ate my first Army chow in Vietnam. It was okay. At dark, we went to bed. We had nothing to do; even so, the adrenaline still flowed and I could not sleep. I was not the only one. Then Ratatat, boom, ratatat, boom . . . ratatat, ratatat. "What the hell is that?" someone in the dark called out.

"Sounds like we're getting hit!"

"It sure does."

"What do we do?"

"Help 'um fight, I guess."

"How? We haven't been issued weapons."

"Somebody go find that sergeant."

I saw a man go out the door in his underwear. In a few minutes, he returned with the sergeant.

"Take it easy, guys. It happens almost every night. If they get anywhere near here, I'll get you up, but for now get some sleep."

"Sleep," a voice said, "How can we sleep with all that shooting going on?"

"You'll get used to it," the sergeant said.

He was right. Gunfire and the sound of helicopters was a constant background noise on the bases in Vietnam.

The next morning, I boarded a C130 cargo plane for a flight to Chu Lai. I had been assigned to the American Division whose headquarters was there.

Already I was impressed with the beauty of Vietnam. We flew up the coast. Jungle lay to my left, and further inland, jungle covered mountains, shaped much like the Appalachians. To my right was the deep-blue ocean with a thin strip of white sand between the blue and green. But gray bomb craters marked the pristine landscape, and there were many. In places, they touched. Blue water filled some.

We landed in Chu Lai. I was glad the flight ended. The C130 is the noisiest airplane on which I have flown. The Army built the base at Chu Lai on the coast around a cove with a beach. That night we slept in a wooden and screen barracks like the one I slept in the night before.

In the night, sirens sounded. We ran to a bunker made of a large culvert pipe covered with sandbags. I cut my head on it. In an hour or so, the all clear sounded. We returned to our beds. The guards had spotted sappers on the beach. They feared they had placed explosives under our barracks.

Next morning after chow, we stood in a pavilion on a hill overlooking our barracks. I saw it rise in the air and slam down in pieces. Then the sound came. Perhaps the sapper's timing device didn't work properly, for it surely would have injured more at night, including injuring or killing me. During the explosion, one soldier was in the building.

I saw my first Medevac helicopter that morning, and I learned to call them DUSTOFFs, an acronym for something. I could not tell how badly the man was hurt or whether he was alive, and I never did hear.

An old Vietnamese man swept the pavilion where we assembled. He wore the traditional straw sampan and his teeth were brown from chewing betel nut. In a mixture of bastardized French and

English he said, "Viet Cong boo coo bad," as he pointed to the carnage.

"No, shit," I said.

The French occupied Vietnam from 1887 to 1949. Many Vietnamese spoke French and were Catholic.

I first heard the term FNG on that day. It means fucking new guy.

We slept in a barracks next to the pile of rubble that had been my barracks the night before. I did not sleep well.

Next day, I flew to Duc Pho in a C7 Caribou, which looked like a scaled-down version of the C130 to me. Duc Pho was the headquarters of the Eleventh Brigade where I was assigned to my company and platoon.

I still held hopes I would be made company clerk or something similar because I was a college graduate. My education did not interest my new commanders in the least. Many college graduates served in the enlisted ranks, not what the media told us back home. In my platoon, one guy had a master's degree, a quarter of us were college graduates, others had some college, and all but one was a high school graduate. The poor and downtrodden were there, but they were not the only ones.

I was relieved to have an M16, helmet, backpack and other combat gear. I remembered my first night in the country and how helpless I felt without a rifle.

"Go to the chopper pad and get on the bird going to San Juan Hill. When you get there, find Captain Yeager," I was told by the First Sergeant. I did as he said. I was on my way to the strange world of combat in Vietnam. . .

29

On the nightly news, I saw soldiers riding in helicopters with their feet hanging out the door, so I knew soldiers rode that way. We did not do it in training. When the UH1 "Huey" arrived, not knowing what to do, I was the last man to board, so I sat with my feet hanging out the door, which was fine until the helicopter went into a steep banked turn and I found myself facing the ground. I grabbed anything I could to prevent falling out. One of the soldiers laughed, then yelled above the roar and chak-chak-chak of the chopper, "Hey, FNG, the centrifugal force will hold you in." It did. Thank God.

We had flown less than fifteen minutes and already we circled Fire Base San Juan Hill. The base sat atop an Appalachian type mountain with two peaks. On one peak there was an artillery battery. Three sides of that peak were a rock cliff. The fourth side connected to the other peak, the home of my infantry battalion. They bulldozed the entire base to tan clay, cleared the jungle on the mountain, and placed several rows of barbed wire around it. The firebase was larger than a football field but much smaller than two.

The mess hall was typical of the Army's wooden buildings in Vietnam with a metal roof and screen above the shortened walls. It sat between the peaks and was the only building on the base. All other structures were bunkers of some sort and covered with sandbags.

The chopper pad sat at the top of the infantry hill. We landed there. All on board went about their business. They left me standing alone, wondering what to do, then I heard, "Hey, FNG, over here."

A soldier walked to me. He looked like all the other soldiers but was the dirtiest I had seen. "I'm Shultz," he said, "Captain Yeager is tied up; he asked me to show you around until he can meet with you." We began to walk down the hill. He pointed and talked. I could tell he enjoyed giving FNGs the tour.

"That rust colored conex with the antenna sticking out of it is our headquarters." Conex is the military's term for shipping container.

"That bunker is the barbershop, and I'm the barber."

"Really, how did you get that job? Were you a barber back in the States?"

"Hell, no, and I'm not gonna lie. I kissed a lot of ass to get it! Somebody's got to do it, and it might as well be me."

Shultz pointed to the left. "That's the shower." A fifty-five gallon barrel sat seven feet in the air on a wooden frame. A shower head protruded from the bottom of the barrel. "You've gotta haul your own water to it. You get it there." He pointed to two water trailers. On one "potable" was painted and "non-potable" on the other. "The potable is for drinking," he said.

"What's that guy over there doing?" I asked.

"Burning shit. That's the latrine."

"Burning shit is exactly what it smells like he is doing," I said. The soldier slid a cut-in-half, metal, fifty-five gallon barrel out the back of the latrine building, poured diesel fuel into it and lit it.

"Sooner or later, you'll have to do it." He pointed across the base. "That bunker over there is the medic. If you need to go on sick call, that's where you go."

Then he pointed to the right and in front of us. "That over there is the four-deuce mortar platoon. What's your MOS?"

"Eleven Charlie."

"Oh, well, then you will probably get to work there when you get senior enough." MOS means your job. Eleven Charlie means mortars.

At Fort Polk, they trained me on the eighty-one and the four-deuce mortars. The four-deuce was larger than the eighty-one. It could not be moved far without a vehicle. The eighty-one can be disassembled and carried in the field by several soldiers. The mortar rounds must also be carried. When we took it on a mission, each man was given a round or a piece of the mortar, adding weight to their already heavy load. They hated it.

The Army designed the eighty-one for trench warfare in World War I, and it is a highly effective weapon under the right circumstances. Carrying it on patrol through the jungle is not the right circumstance.

"Here's what's gonna happen," Shultz said. "You will mostly work as an eleven bravo, rifleman.

Sometimes, you will take the eighty-one out in the field with you, but not much. There's not much need for it when you have artillery and air cover. Hell, the fight will be over before you can get the damn thing set up. This ain't World War II. It gets in the way, in my opinion."

He continued, "Platoons are small, fifteen men or so. You will stay out patrolling the jungle for three weeks, then return to the base and pull bunker guard for one week, and then go out again."

"Three weeks!" I said.

"Three weeks," he said.

"No bath for three weeks," I said.

"No bath for three weeks unless you can find a stream, and you are sure it is safe, but why bother. You ain't gonna have a date. Nobody is out there in the jungle except the enemy and us."

"God, I'll bet everybody stinks."

"You know; it's funny. When you are out in the field, you can't smell each other. But if you are clean and you get around someone who has spent three weeks in the field, you can hardly stand the stench. A platoon coming in off mission smells so bad they will make you sick at your stomach."

"The other hill is artillery hill. We never go up there. You will sleep in that bunker over there with your platoon." He pointed to it. "And that over there is the movie theater." He pointed to an amphitheater made in the side of infantry hill with wooden benches and an outdoor movie screen.

"Do they show new movies?"

"Pretty much, they're a few months old."

"Have they shown *Alice's Restaurant?*"

"No way, the Army will never show that movie!"   *Alice's Restaurant* was a popular antiwar movie. I didn't know then, but I had stumbled on to a standing joke on San Juan Hill. When someone asked, "What's the movie tonight?" *Alice's Restaurant* was the answer you gave when you didn't know. Later, to everyone's surprise, they did show it.

"Here comes Captain Yeager," Shultz said. I did not know then, but I was about to meet the most capable Army officer I knew in my brief military career. He was not much older than me, twenty-seven or so. Yeager was from somewhere in the Midwest. This tour of duty was his second in Vietnam. He knew how to get the job done and keep us from getting killed while doing it, and he knew how to keep the idiots he worked for off our back, which was important. Strategy and tactics fit nicely in a book. Combat experience does not. My guess is, the battalion commander was a book guy. Leadership matters. Command miscalculations are, have always been, and always will be, the number-one killer of soldiers.

Colin Powell was somewhere in the upper end of the chain of command. He later became the Chairman of the Joint Chiefs of Staff, Secretary of State, and a hero for his planning of the Gulf War. Some wanted him to run for president. Photographs of our commanders hung on our company headquarters wall. I noticed Powell because he was black. There were few black officers then. I hadn't seen one, but in my low post, I didn't see many officers.

After a salute and a greeting, Yeager began to explain what he expected of me. What Shultz told me was right.

Except for the black captain's bars sewn on his collar, Yeager was indistinguishable from the rest of us, but his manner left no doubt he was in charge. Probably I still had the "deer in the headlights" look. That is how I felt. When he heard my accent, he asked where I was from. I told him. "Good," he said, "Southerners make good soldiers."

"We do have that reputation, sir," I said.

I learned that San Juan Hill had not been attacked in anyone's memory. The cliffs protected the artillery hill, high ground and good vision at the infantry end made it hard to attack. The base sat alone in unpopulated jungle with no road to it. No towns were close by. All supplies came by chopper. As firebases go, San Juan Hill was relatively safe when I was there.

Captain Yeager explained, "In our area of operation, there are no civilians. It's a free-fire zone. The population has been moved to the coast. There are no villages, no farms. Anyone out there other than us is either Viet Cong or NVA. They have no other reason to be there. Nixon's incursion into Cambodia really helped us. They don't have the supplies for a prolonged fight any longer. Don't misunderstand, we still get hit, but it's all guerilla tactics out there now." He pointed to the jungle.

"Come on, I will introduce you to the guys." We walked to an eighty-one mortar pit, but there was no mortar in it. The guys in my platoon sat on a sandbag wall that surrounded the pit.

This moment was an important one. Trust is as vital as food to a soldier. I needed to gain these men's trust, and I prayed they were worthy of mine.

In past wars, men trained as units and deployed together. In Vietnam, we served alone. Comradery is the glue that binds man to man and builds strong combat units. Men will die for their brothers, but sacrificing yourself for a stranger is more difficult. The planners of this war forgot that. I felt alone.

My platoon looked more like Pancho Villa's banditos than soldiers in Uncle Sam's army, with headbands, hair, and mustaches too long for military regulations, but they were all clean-shaven, they had just bathed. They looked war-hardened. My eyes widened, filled with admiration, fear, and wonder. Could I measure up? . . .

30

Again, my feet hung out a Huey's door. This was my first mission. I didn't know what to expect. I didn't understand why we were going wherever we were going or what we were going to do when we got there. All on board seemed to know but me. I now know the other soldiers didn't know either. They were just used to not knowing. I heard someone say something about "search and destroy."

Twenty minutes into the flight, the door gunner began to fire his M-60 machine gun. The hot brass ejected from it and landed on me. One spent shell went down the back of my shirt. It burned.

Confusion . . . rockets fired from and adjacent gunship, *Fear* . . . were we going into a hot landing zone? *Noise* . . . intensified my fear, the Huey's clack, clack, the M-60's rapid bang, and the hiss of the rockets as they shot by. . . the explosions when they hit the ground. The sudden inflow of deadly images crashed together in me. *Overwhelmed . . . what's happening?* We landed. I jumped out, ran away from the chopper and dove to the ground, eyes ahead, ears listening . . . I heard nothing except a voice, "Get up FNG, it ain't a hot LZ."

"Then why did they do all that shooting?"

"Sometimes they do that just to keep 'um honest."

"I wish somebody had told me," I said.

"Hell, I wish somebody told me! I didn't know they were going to do that either."

"I forgot your name."

"Rinehart."

"I forgot yours."

"McCoy."

"Where you from, Rinehart?"

"Atlanta."

"You?"

"Greenville, South Carolina."

"Good."

Capitan Yeager called out, "Saddle up, men. Let's go see what's on that mountain." By now the sun rose above it. We began our march.

No sweat, I'm in shape, I thought. At noon, we stopped to eat. I said to McCoy, "You guys always, *huff, huff,* march that hard."

"You'll get used to it."

I pulled a C-ration can from my pack, poured ham and lima beans from it into my canteen cup, and began heating it with an Army issued heat tab as we were taught in basic training. I noticed McCoy didn't bother. He opened his can with the little p38 can opener that came with the C-rations and ate it cold from the can.

"That heat tab ain't worth a shit. Here, try this." He took a block of C-4 explosive from his pack, cut off a piece and rolled it into a ball. "Light that. It won't explode." I did as he said while thinking it might be a gag. It burned a rapid white-hot fire. In seconds, it warmed my ham and lima beans.

"The Army has a new ration called a lurp. They're pretty good but we hardly ever get any. The REMFs steal 'um for their midnight snacks, same with the good cigarettes. All we get is fucking Pall Mall out here," McCoy said. The Army supplied cartons of cigarettes to soldiers in the field, and C-rations contained small packs in them as well.

"What's a REMF?"

"Rear echelon mother fucker."

He looked at my pack. "The way you've got that thing packed is fucked up. Let me give you some finer points of this business. Put your extra clothes at the bottom of your pack. You probably aren't going to need them anyway. Then pack your poncho and poncho liner. Put the C-rations on top of that, then your grenades, claymore, bandoliers of ammo, and the M-60 ammo on top of that." We each carried a belt of ammo for the M-60 machinegun. Soldiers lugged about eighty-five pounds of gear with them all day, every day.

"I know you are tired, but the next time you sit down, don't flop down like you just did. Look first, or you might get a bungee stick up your ass," he said. A bungee stick is a foot-long sliver of sharpened bamboo stuck in the ground along a trail where American soldiers were likely to take a break. Often, they were dipped in feces to cause infection. "Sit on one and your war is over," McCoy said.

"Thanks for the warning," I said. *Good, I think I have a mentor,* I thought.

We walked through the jungle. The plants looked as if God put genetic traits in a bowl and jumbled them, then pulled them out as in a lottery. Trees with oak-like bark grew pine-like needles. A maple-looking tree decorated itself with white flowers, and a bush that looked like a blackberry bush produced red berries. Wild banana trees grew in the jungle, and a strange tree grew a cherry-looking fruit out from its bark in rings around its trunk. I had never seen anything like that.

I heard bird sounds. They reminded me of Tarzan movies. An insect made a sound like a two-stroke motorcycle engine running in the distance. We called them Yamaha bugs.

That night, McCoy and I bedded together. He tied his poncho's corners to bushes to make a tent. I laid my poncho on the ground for a ground cloth. The rest built shelters in the same way. I used my extra clothes for a pillow and my poncho liner for a blanket.

"Why do we need this poncho liner? It's hot as hell here," I said. A poncho liner is a lightweight polyester coverlet.

"You'll see," McCoy said.

At dark the mosquitoes came, and the poncho liner went over my head, leaving a hole for my nose. I could hear them biting it over my ear. In Vietnam, I learned to sleep anywhere and under any conditions, including the driving rain.

On my third or fourth mission, Captain Yeager brought a jungle hammock, which is a hammock with a tent-like covering. Rather than lie on it, you get in it. Sleeping hanging in the air is not a good idea in a war zone, but we were deep in the jungle. Captain Yeager was confident we would not be attacked.

At night we took turns on guard duty. The shift lasted an hour and there were two men awake at all times. McCoy woke me for my turn. I stood to shake off the drowsiness. When I was fully awakened, I sat by McCoy, staring into the jungle, rifle in hand.

I heard a rustling in the bushes. Then they moved. I woke McCoy. I whispered, "Look," and pointed. McCoy watched. They moved again. He grabbed his rifle and rolled into firing position. I lay ready, nearby. *This is it, my first fight.* The adrenaline flowed. I was too scared to be afraid. *This is it. I might not survive the night.*

"What do you think it is?" I whispered.

He answered in a voice so slight that it almost could not be heard, "I'm not sure."

The bushes move again.

"Shoot that mother fucker," McCoy yelled. We fired, *boom, boom.*

An ape jumped from the bush, ran over McCoy and me, jumped on Captain Yeager's jungle hammock, and swung it around a few times, dumping Captain Yeager on the ground. I relaxed. We were too stunned to laugh that night, but later we did. Later the whole platoon laughed over beers, and Captain Yeager never used the jungle hammock again.

31

"There are three rules for jungle warfare: Don't let the enemy smell you before he hears you. Don't let the enemy hear you before he sees you, and don't let him see you at all." An old jungle fighter told me that at a pub in London. He was a veteran of Britain's fighting in Burma during World War II. By now I knew the enemy. I was becoming an old guy who tutored the FNGs as they came to Vietnam behind me.

Most days were Boy Scout days, hiking, camping, joking, but always there was fear, the fear that the truth would hit us like lightning from nowhere to remind us of why we were in beautiful Vietnam.

Echo Company usually went out alone, but on this day we worked with Delta Company. They walked in line in front of us. I noticed three rocks stacked one on top of the other as we entered an old rice paddy.

"Tell'um to wait," I said.

"Why?" McCoy said.

"Look." I pointed to the three rocks.

"So what?"

"That's a sign the Viet Cong use to warn other Viet Cong there is a booby trap ahead."

"Where'd you hear that?"

"Fort Polk."

"You sure, I never heard anything about . . ."

Boom, we heard an explosion, then the distinct rat, tat, tat, of AK-47s, then the lower sound of M-16s returning fire.

We hit the ground.

"Come on, we better low-crawl to the front to help'um out," McCoy said.

We crawled ahead, but the firing stopped. When we reached the front, the Delta Company medic bandaged the man injured in the booby trap. Blood soaked through the bandages as quickly as he put them on. Within twenty minutes, a medevac chopper came. The wounded man's friends loaded him on it.

We camped with Delta Company that night. I noticed their company medic carried a Bible but no weapon. He read it until the sun set, and I wondered about him. No one spoke to him. The men of Delta Company didn't like him. He was different, but I admired his courage. No doubt he was a true conscientious objector, so many who claimed to be were not.

I believed that in the antiwar movement back in the States, some who claimed they didn't believe in war, in truth were afraid, and they justified their fear by declaring themselves pacifists. They claimed the moral high ground, but they didn't have it. Fate will not let them off. There are times when one must fight. Evil must be confronted, and evil does exist.

Communism degenerates to tyranny as people are forced to conform to its dictates. It cannot work without a heavy hand. The question was not a moral one, but one of practicality. How much American blood and treasure were we willing to spend in Vietnam? At what point was it just not worth it?

In my time in Vietnam, the war was effectively won. The Communist gained victory on the streets of America as America worked against itself, not in the jungles of Vietnam. Had we persevered, the South Vietnamese might have prospered as the South Korean's have. The contrast between freedom and tyranny is stark on the Korean peninsula.

OUR DUTY CYCLE repeated itself. We spent an easy week guarding San Juan Hill. Echo Company was to spend the next three weeks patrolling the jungle as usual. Colonel Grimes, the battalion commander, decided he would go with us. The companies of the Eleventh Brigade were to work closely together under his command. He told us to bring the eighty-one mortar. I had been in the country for six months, and this was only the second time we had taken it. The last time I had fired one was at Fort Polk.

The helicopters dropped the entire battalion, one helicopter at a time into a small landing zone cut on the top of a hill in the jungle. Our door gunner was nervous. "This is taking too long. If there were any Vietcong down there, we would have drawn fire by now," he said.

It was a short walk to our camp site. Colonel Grimes sent each company to a different place. All were close by on hilltops. Charlie Company was the closest, in shouting distance. The Army had used our camp site before. A mortar pit was already built on it. We set our eighty-one up. The jungle was cut back just enough to fire it.

Colonel Grimes sent three men to set a mech on the trail we had just used. In military jargon mech means mechanized ambush, a booby trap. He sent a list of coordinates to the mortar platoon. He wanted a round fired at each coordinate that evening after dark.

Richard Hass sat with a poncho draped over him doing fire direction calculations for the mortar shots. He used a flashlight with a red lens, not good conditions for calculating. Richard was a psychology major from Indiana University, and I liked him.

At night, any light gave away our position. If we smoked, we lit our cigarettes under a poncho and cupped them with our hands to cover the red glow. My hands always smelled of tobacco.

Richard brought his calculations to Sergeant Daily, the gunner. He sighted the mortar. Richard stopped him. "I don't like this. That's too close to Charlie Company. Hang on. I'm going to ask Colonel Grimes to cancel this shot," and he went to find him.

"Fire it," he said when he returned. "Colonel Grimes said he has got it all figured out."

Mortar rounds have eight bags of explosive propellant charges attached around the base of them. The number of bags left attached to the round determines the distance it will travel. Except for the maximum range, setting the distance requires removing some of the bags. Charge one means one bag; charge two means two bags and so forth. Richard had determined the charge as part of his calculations

I was the ammo man, the easiest job of all on a mortar team. I took a mortar round from a stack of them and handed it to Sergeant Daily, the assistant gunner.

"What charge?" he asked.

"Charge one."

Daily began to remove the unneeded bags. When he finished, there were no bags on the round. "Hey, hey, that's not right. That's not charge one." I said.

"What do you know? As far as I'm concerned, you're still a fucking new guy." He dropped the round down the barrel.

Poomp, it sounded like someone quickly pulled a plug from a big jug rather than the usual bang as only the ignition charge fired, but it was enough to launch the round.

"That didn't sound right," someone said. Time stopped. The round hung in the air. We heard it explode, then the screams began, the screams of dying men. The screams I still hear. Someone called out, "Stop firing you are hitting Charlie Company. Stop, stop, stop, goddamnit, stop, you are hitting Charlie Company." All of us stood looking toward the sounds.

No one spoke. For the longest time, no one spoke.

The round killed five . . . five, five, five . . . five good Americans dead, muerto . . . fucking gone, out of the game.

That night I slept near a rotting log. It smelled of decay. The dark eyes in the dark places in the jungle called to me, "Hey, Rick, where is the honor? Where is the glory? Hey, Rick, where is Audi Murphy? Where is John Wayne?" I sat up. I threw up, then I stood up and looked up through the jungle at the moon. It too said, "Hey, Rick, where is the honor? Where is the glory? What's the matter big boy? You don't like war?"

I felt a click in my head. The click was physical; something I had never felt, something in my brain moved, and I knew it changed me.

Next morning, Colonel Grimes' radioman called out, "Charlie Company is coming up our hill. Don't fire'em up." Then he screamed, "Colonel Grimes, you had the men put a mech on the trail last night! They aren't coming that way. Are they?"

Without being told to do so, the radio man screamed into his handset." Stop, Stop, hold your position. Don't take another step." Colonel Grimes grabbed the first soldier he saw, "You take two men with you and go back down there and disarm that mech we put up last night."

"Sir, I don't know where it is."

"Find the men who put it out."

"Yes, sir." But it was too late. The mech exploded. The radio was silent, but when Charlie Company reached us they carried a body with them. A third of their company was dead, none at the hand of the enemy.

The man who carried the body over his shoulders dropped it on the ground in front of Colonel Grimes, then attacked him with his K-Bar knife, trying to slit his throat. He knocked Colonel Grimes to the ground and they struggled. Why he didn't just shoot him, I don't know. Others in his platoon pulled him off. "There has been enough death," one said. The man dropped his K-Bar, his friends still held him. He took long and hard breaths, keeping his eyes on Colonel Grimes until his friends led him away. No charges were brought against him. I don't know if the Army investigated the incidents of that mission. No one ever talked to me and I saw it all. I had touched the round that killed five Americans.

I think Sergeant Daily purposefully tried to make the round fall short of Charlie Company by firing it with no charges on it, but I was told Richard made a mistake in his calculations. It should have been charge two not one. Richard blamed himself. I told him what I thought happened, but he still blamed himself, and I wonder what toll it has taken on him in his later life.

I no longer trusted Colonel Grimes and I thanked God Captain Yeager lay between me and him in the chain of command. Strategy and tactics can be learned from books, but the ability to think quickly and properly under the stress of combat is a gift from God.

When we returned to San Juan Hill, several letters waited. One was from Travis. I read it:

Dear Rick,

It's over, the wedding of the century. Well, maybe not quite that, but it was a good one. Everything went well. I am a married man now, with a wife, an apartment, and a dog. The only thing missing is a kid, and we are going to wait a while for that.

My Dad was my best man. I would have asked you to do the honor, but rumor has it you are otherwise occupied. Jake, Rodney, Jay, Steve, and Lankford were my groomsmen. Eileen, Linda, Bonnie, Carol, and Jane were the bridesmaids. Marianne was the maid-of-honor or whatever you call it. I don't know. I left all that wedding stuff to Nancy and her mom.

Believe me, weddings are for women. When you take the plunge, go fishing and let the women do whatever they want. That way you will be happy, so will your girl.

Nothing went wrong in the ceremony. No one dropped the ring or forgot to say I do. Everyone looked nice in the tux that we got from your old man's place. I would describe the women's dresses, but I know you couldn't care less, but I must say Nancy was stunning.

The reception was at West Lake Country Club, complete with a cornball band. Everyone had a good time dancing, especially when the band played Rolling on the River.

Jake came with Alice. Nancy's mom wanted me to ask Jake to get a haircut for the wedding, but I didn't do it. He is still in Carrollton working at the Bay Station. Marianne came with some Georgia Tech grad. He is a pilot in the Air Force now. I guess that makes sense since her Dad is a pilot. He was okay, but it just didn't seem right. She belongs with you.

Nancy and I will start teaching this fall. For now, I am working in a carpet mill. Anyway, keep your head down and come back in one piece. Write soon. We love you,

Travis

I walked into an empty bunker to rest. It was dark and cooler inside. Someone left his pack on the dirt floor. A cassette player sat beside the pack with a tape in it. I sat on the floor near it, then punched the play button and remembered the night Marianne and I made love to the sounds that now filled the bunker. The *Crosby, Stills and Nash* album played, and I wanted her, and I wanted my old life back, and I cried. I cried but no one saw me. . . .

32

Who am I? What am I? I'm in this dark place, and it wants to kill my mother's me and spawn a new creature with fangs and claws. My mother's me is the better me. If war defines me, then I am a warrior, and I can be nothing else. We need such men. Am I one?

Those who will not fight live by the liege of those who will, and they live in the delusion that this is not so. Safety gives room for lofty thoughts, and humanity walks toward God on thoughts.

But in my war, I can live and still be dead; my mother's me gone. The body breathes, but God's creation has departed, as sure as if there were an arrow shot through its heart. I do not want this. I

will go to the line but I will not cross it. This war
will not kill my body or my mother's me.

    We patrolled. Captain Yeager commanded as usual. McCoy walked point, and I followed him. The day was a casual day, almost carefree. I don't know why, but we felt safe, no sense of impending doom, no feeling that the enemy was near. We laughed. We joked. We were too loud. We walked in line, one behind the other.

    "Hang on; I'm stuck in a "wait-a-minute-vine," someone in the column behind called out as he freed himself from a pesky jungle entanglement. McCoy, me and Stokes, the man who walked behind me did not stop. Stokes was a sniper and he carried an M21 sniper rifle. The distance grew between us and the rest more than we intended.

    We came to a ravine, and near it the foliage changed. "It looks like home," I said, and it did look like the Georgia wood, not a Georgia pine woods, but one of hardwoods, oaks, hickory, and such as in the North Georgia mountains, and dry leaves covered the ground. I had not seen a place like this in the usually wet jungle.

    "Listen." From the bottom of the ravine, we could hear the roar from a waterfall and through the bushes see it a little. I thought about my father and family trips to North Georgia and several waterfalls we saw together as a family in love.

We stepped into the ravine, but we did not step on firm earth. Leaves were packed against the edge of the ravine, and they gave way under our weight, and we fell, rolling down the side of the ravine in the leaves like laughing children, and in the creek also laughing like children, three Viet Cong were playing, devoid of most of their clothing. They could not hear us for the noise of the waterfall.

"Look," I said to McCoy. By now the rest caught us, sliding in the leaves as we did and laughing. Captain Yeager saw the Viet Cong. "Spread out," he said and motioned with his hands. "You guys get the first one. You guys the second one and you the last." McCoy, Stokes, and I aimed at the first man, an easy shot for us, especially Stokes. "When I give the command, fire," Captain Yeager said.

I put my rifle to my shoulder. It shook. *I don't want to do this.* In the jungle ahead, there were dark places and they seemed to have eyes, and from the sun above I felt as if I were being watched. *I don't want to do this.* The man in my sights played as I liked to do. *I don't want to do this.*

Get it together, Rick; he would kill you without blinking an eye . . . He's vicious, but he's so damn helpless now. I thought war was kill or be killed, a fair fight. If only I had been here long enough to learn to hate . . . If I had seen a friend die at their hand, revenge would burn in me and I could fulfill Karma's circle. At least I could justify myself that way. At least I could say . . . "the mother fucker deserved to die." Maybe he did, but I see his young face. He's human. I don't want to do this.

"Fire."

I did my duty. . . A communist lay dead, and a mother's son lay dead and a brother lay dead. . . Dead. The dark jungle's eyes taunted the light. "He's ours now," they said. *No, I'm not. You will not take me*, but no light peeked through the canopy. Where was God?

I once heard the story about a Samurai. His lord ordered him to execute a captured enemy. He raised his sword, and as he did the enemy spat on him. The Samurai sheathed his sword and would not kill him. To kill in anger was against his code. To me anger was the fuel I needed. To kill, hate is your friend. I felt neither. I was not the only one to shoot. My hands shook as I squeezed the trigger. Perhaps I missed, and will it matter to God when I stand before him?

33

"Rinehart, Rinehart." Someone shook me.

I woke up to see the ugly face of a soldier with crooked teeth staring at me. He was an FNG. I didn't remember his name.

"What?" I said.

"Captain Yeager wants to see you. He's waiting."

"We've been looking all over for you. Why did you sleep in here?"

"Where am I? What the hell, do you want?" The FNG looked confused.

"Duc Pho," he said. "You don't remember?"

"Yeah, yeah, now I do." *God my head hurts.*

"Why did you sleep in here?'

"There wasn't room in the other barracks. That's why, dumb-ass. Give me a minute." I sat on the bed with my feet on the floor and my head resting in my hands. I remembered that we were in Duc Pho. I remembered the Filipino band at the enlisted club and the beer. *What a night.* Then I remembered Kim and Carter and his heroin. I remembered crawling into this empty barracks and I remembered the mosquitos that feasted on me before I found the dirty poncho liner to cover myself.

Was it a dream? It was so real. They say when you die, your life passes before your eyes seconds. It was like that. The whole story came to me, Jake, Travis, Nancy, and Marianne. "Marianne," I said her name out loud. *God did I fuck that up.*

I stood and stumbled catching myself by putting my hand on the wall. *Oh, God, my head.* I brushed the paste out of my mouth and the stale beer taste, straightened my uniform as best I could. I didn't want Captain Yeager to see me like this. I hoped I still didn't smell like beer. *What a night!*

I found Captain Yeager outside the mess hall.

"Rinehart, there is an opening in the four-deuce mortar platoon. You are senior mortar man now. You want to finish out your tour of duty there?"

"Yes, sir, I do."

"Good God Rinehart, you look like you got hit by a bus. Go get you some breakfast. Report to Sergeant Deyampert when we get back to San Juan Hill."

"Yes, Sir." With his words, my war changed. San Juan Hill was safe compared to the jungle. I had seven weeks left and I knew I would make it.

One of my buddies in Echo Company teased me. "Think you're getting over like a fat rat, don't you, Rinehart?"

"Yeah, well, a little bit. It's just the luck of the draw."

"You might not feel so lucky once you get there."

"Why?"

"You will be the only white guy in the platoon. Monk and his buddies run off every white guy they transfer there."

"Who the hell is Monk."

"He's kinda the ringleader. He's big, black, and mean," he said.

When Echo Company left for the jungle, I stayed behind.

Race relations in Vietnam were bad, reflecting race relations in America during the early seventies. I worried. *Monk can't be as bad as the Viet Cong,* I thought. *At least, he won't try to kill me. . . I think?*

I walked in the door of the four-deuce bunker. Monk was the only one there. He listened to Miles Davis on his cassette player.

"Don't tell me they are going to try another honky- ass white boy in here?" he said.

"Don't tell me you just called me Honky, motherfucker. If you want to play racial slur, I got a few I can throw at you myself."

I knew better than to be weak, but Monk was frightening. I doubted he would hurt me. His tactics were all psychological, but two could play at that game.

He pointed to a bunk. "Throw your shit over there. I'll give you a week before you are begging to get out of here." He mumbled something about pussy-ass white boys under his breath. I couldn't fully hear it and let it pass.

Then he said. "I don't know why you white boys are so fucking afraid of me. This motherfucker from Idaho ran out of here crying for a transfer. Said he'd rather fight in the jungle than live with me and my brothers.

"Well, Monk, if you don't want people to be afraid of you, quit scaring the shit out of them." I set my gear at the end of my bunk, pulled back the mosquito net, and lay down.

"You like fried chicken?" I asked.

"Yeah," Monk said before he considered the question.

"That's a racist. Next you'll be asking me if I like watermelon."

"Me, too," I said. "You like black-eyed peas and sweet potatoes?"

"What do you care what the fuck I like."

"Just curious, you like'um?"

"Yeah, I like black-eyed peas and sweet potatoes," he said slowly. "So the fuck what?"

"I like'em, too, and I like Miles Davis."

"What does your white-ass know about Miles Davis? I thought you white boys listened to The Beatles and dumb shit like that. What's that other one? Creedence Clearwater Revival. Yeah, Creeeedence," he said in his base voice, "and dumb shit like that."

"I used to work with this older black guy. He listened to jazz on the radio all day long. I picked it up from him. That's the *Kind of Blue Album you are playing*. I know that much."

"A fucking classic," he said.

"Sure is."

"Where you from?" he asked

"Atlanta."

"Me, too, what part.?"

We had grown up about four miles apart, but Atlanta was a segregated city in those days. After a few minutes of silence, Monk said, "You like pigs' feet."

"Never tried'em."

"I rest my case."

"You like Otis Redding?" I asked.

"Yeah."

"Me, too, ever see him?"

"Last time he was in Atlanta before I got drafted," he said.

"I was there," I said.

"That was a black crowd."

"I noticed that, but I was in it."

There was silence again. "You like chitterlings?"

"No."

"See there, motherfucker." He turned away and said no more.

Monk did not welcome me as his brother, but he did accept me, and with his blessing, I had no trouble with the other blacks in the platoon. I began relearning mortars from them, but I really didn't care about it. I was going home soon.

I had been in the platoon two weeks when Monk said, "I got a whole five-gallon bucket of pink paint."

"Where did you get pink paint up here?"

"Found it in a bunker they use as a storeroom."

"Why would anyone have pink paint in the middle of the jungle?"

"Your guess is as good as mine, but I know one thing. The inside of this bunker is gonna be pink as a pussy tonight."

That night, the platoon began painting the bunker's interior pink. I don't remember where we got the paint brushes.

But while painting, I began to feel sick, feverous, and chilled.

"Monk, man, I gotta lay down," I said. He mumbled something about shamming-ass white boy. After a few minutes, he pulled back the mosquito net, "Damn, man, you look like shit. I didn't think you could get any paler, but you have."

"We got a blanket or extra poncho liner? I'm freezing."

In a few minutes, Monk threw a poncho liner over me. "Man," he said, "looks like you got malaria to me. Better go on sick call in the morning." I could tell he was concerned.

"I took those fucking malaria pills every morning like they told me to."

Then I remembered the mosquitoes that had feasted on me in Duc Pho two weeks ago. I knew the incubation period for malaria was two weeks, and I feared Monk was right.

Next morning, the fever was gone. I was weak, and it felt as if something was in my eye. I went to the medic's bunker. He took a blood sample and sent it to be tested for malaria.

"It will take a few days to get the results. Let me look at your eye." He examined my eye. "There is a lesion in it." He gave me several small tubes of ointment. Next day, it was worse and the next worse.

I went back to get the results of my malaria test. "We don't know what caused your fever, but we do know you don't have malaria," he said.

"Doc, you know in the Bible Jesus talks about having a beam in your eye. That is exactly what it feels like. I can't keep it open, especially in the light."

He looked at it. "It's worse. I'm going to send you to Duc Pho to let them have a look at it."

At Duc Pho, a doctor shined his penlight in it. "Soldier, I don't see a thing in your eye. You wouldn't try to get out of duty. Would you? You're shamming. I'm going to send you back to the field." *Fuck you, you stupid son of a bitch.*

"Respectfully, sir, I can barely keep it open. Anybody can see that."

He was angry that I challenged him. "Most people can close one eye. I don't see a thing wrong with it. Come here, Sam. Do you see anything in this man's eye?" He called to another doctor who was walking down the hall. The other doctor looked at it.

"It looks to me like there is a lesion in it. Better send him to the ophthalmologist in Chu Lai," he said then walked away.

The first doctor's face tensed. I saw his anger but he hid it from his colleague.

"You report to me when you get back from Chu Lai," he said.

"Yes, sir," I said with a smile and a smirk, but thought *I ain't reporting to jack shit.*

He angrily wrote an order for me to travel to the ophthalmologist in Chu Lai. I took it and left.

35

I sat in the air terminal at Duc Pho awaiting a military flight to Chu Lai. The terminal was a twelve by sixteen-foot wooden building with a counter at one end, and two-by-four benches built around the walls. Inside, it was dark except for a dim light shining down on a soldier who leaned on the counter. The soldier waited. He did no work. Gray light of the overcast day came to the open door but stopped there, as if it were not allowed inside.

My eye hurt as I stared from the dark into the light, but the pain was worth it. That's where she stood awaiting her eyes to adjust to the darkness. She removed her sampan, the traditional conical straw hat the Vietnamese have worn for the past three-thousand years. She walked to the counter, "Please, sir, I need to go to Chu Lai," she said in perfect English as she gave the soldier her papers. She wore a white brocade traditional ao dai, which is a long-sleeve tunic with ankle-length panels at front and back, worn over matching trousers.

By her dress, I knew she came from a well-to-do family. She walked from the counter and sat across from me. I said hello.

"Hello," she returned the greeting in her soft voice, then smiled and that was all it took. I was smitten. Our plane arrived, a Caribou. We were the only passengers.

A Caribou can accommodate thirty-two passengers, but the loadmaster had set up the cabin for cargo. He seated us next to one another on webbed seats along the wall. *Perfect,* I thought.

"My name is Rick," I said as I thought, s*he's so small, so beautiful. I am a run of the mill soldier, a big oaf, a dime a dozen. I am not worthy of her and never will be.*

"My name is Anh." She cupped her long Vietnamese hair with her hand to make it hang at her back.

"Your English is so good."

"I learned in school. I speak French, English, Chinese, and Vietnamese."

"Oh, wow. I can barely speak one language."

"May I ask why you are on a military flight?"

"My father is a government official. My brother was in a movie theater when the Viet Cong threw a hand grenade into the crowd. He is in the US military hospital at Chu Lai. I am going to see him."

"I am so sorry. Was he badly hurt?"

"Yes, I pray he will live. I am a Catholic."

"I pray he will live, too.

For a few moments, there was only the sound of the engines as I in my own way did say a prayer for her brother.

"I am going to the same hospital for my eye."

"I noticed that you have it closed. I thought that might be why you were traveling."

"Yeah, I don't know what is wrong. I can't keep it open. It's so sensitive to light. I am to see the ophthalmologist there."

The flight from Duc Pho is not a long one, perhaps a half hour. We chatted the entire time. When we separated, she walked away with the same grace in which she had arrived, and I felt empty. She was not for me, just a chance encounter, but when she was gone, I felt alone.

I watched her get into an officer's jeep. I had been with a gentlewoman, an accomplished lady. I lived in an ugly world. She lived in the same world, but her grace took her above it. She touched my life at a time when I had forgotten grace existed, and I knew I would never forget her.

In Chu Lai someone gave me a ride to the outpatient barracks. It sat just off the beach and there was an Enlisted Man's Club nearby. *What more could I want? There was a beach that rivals those in the Caribbean for beauty, hot chow, beer, and at the Enlisted Man's Club that night, a band was scheduled to play. The only thing missing was girls in bikinis.*

I found a bed, hung out with the other soldiers in the outpatient barracks, then went to chow with them. After chow, we walked down to the beach. A few soldiers lay in the evening sun with uniforms stripped as far as they could go while maintaining military decorum, with shirts and boots off, pants rolled up to the knees. A few played in the water.

"How does the hospital know I'm here?" I asked a soldier who had lived in the outpatient barracks for a few weeks.

"They don't."

"Good. My eye doesn't hurt. I just can't keep it open. I'm going to take a day at the beach before I report to the hospital."

"If I were you, I would do exactly that."

I went to the Enlisted Man's Club and began drinking beer that afternoon and continued into the night. The band began playing at eight, a Filipino band as usual, by nine-thirty, all were rowdy drunk. A black soldier and a white soldier argued about the song the band should play next. The black wanted an Otis Redding song played, the white guy one by The Doors.

They began a drunken brawl, but only managed a few punches when, *boom,* there was a flash of light, the building shook and the electricity went off. All ran to the door, and the cover of a nearby bunker, their grievances forgotten. The party was over. A rocket had exploded on the beach just outside the club. It made me angry. *I can't have a beer without those son of a bitches trying to kill me. Fuck it. I'm going to bed.*

In the morning, I awoke early and with a hangover. I wanted coffee. The mess hall was close and I could smell bacon cooking. The aroma drew me out of bed and to the mess hall.

After breakfast, I walked on a sidewalk that paralleled the beach. High dunes blocked my view of the ocean, and from the top of one, a man stumbled down like a drunk and collided with me. Together we fell to the ground.

"Sorry," he said. "The dune was steeper than I thought."

He wasn't drunk and he didn't make me angry. I laughed.

"That's okay. My hangover and I forgive you," I said. He walked beside me. His name tag had O'Neal embroidered on it.

"I'm looking for somebody from Tennessee. You know anybody from Tennessee around here? Do you?"

"No, I don't know anybody around here, period. I'm from the outpatient barracks."

"Is there anybody in the mess hall? I gotta find somebody from Tennessee." He sounded desperate.

"No, it's early. Nobody much is in there yet."

"Why have you gotta find someone from Tennessee?"

"My boss is a *Stars and Stripes* reporter. He wants to interview someone from Tennessee."

"You work for *Stars and Stripes*?"

"No, I'm his bodyguard."

"I didn't know reporters had bodyguards."

"Most don't, but this one is a Senator's son."

"Let me guess, he's from Tennessee."

"Right, he is Senator Al Gore's son, Al Junior."

We continued walking together. "You've got a southern accent. Where are you from?"

"Georgia."

"That's right next door. Maybe you'll do. It doesn't look like I'm going to find anybody from Tennessee around here. You want to be interviewed by a *Stars and Stripes* reporter?"

"Why not, I've got nothing else to do. We walked over the dunes to the beach and to Al Gore. I had no idea I was meeting a future Presidential candidate and Vice President of the United States.

Al Gore is a big man. He stood. I looked up to him and I do not look up to many men. Four others sat at his feet. O'Neal introduced me. I shook his hand. It was open and limp. "You from Tennessee?" he said.

"No, Georgia."

O'Neal interrupted, "He's the only one around."

Gore sat down, and I joined his group. I expected him to interview me, but he asked no questions, nor did he join the small talk the others made. He stared at the ocean.   Except for O'Neal, I felt everything those in his entourage said was calculated to impress him. I didn't care. I wasn't impressed. I had known a Senator's son in college. He was a regular guy, and I expected Al to be the same. *Probably went to the University of Tennessee,* I thought. I had friends there. *Maybe he knows them.*

"Al, where did you go to college?"

"Harvard."

"No shit, big time."

Well, we have nothing in common. Harvard people and regular people live in different worlds.

"I went to West Georgia College."

"Oh." He looked away, uninterested.

Fuck this jerkoff.

Every soldier knew his ETS date. It was the day he would leave Vietnam, and no conversation between newly introduced soldiers went long before someone asked, "When do you ETS?" All had mentioned theirs but Al, so I asked,

"Al, when do you ETS?"

"I've applied to divinity school," he said.

"So what does that have to do with your ETS date? You can't go home because you applied to a school. If you could, everybody would do that."

"You can, if you get accepted to divinity school."

"Really, why?"

"That's the law."

"I never knew that. Where are you going to school?"

"Vanderbilt."

"When do you leave?"

"I'm not sure, soon."

"Cool, how long have you been here?"

He's not open like a regular soldier. He doesn't want to talk about this, I thought.

"Not too long, but longer than I want."

He drew his knees to his chest and looked at the ocean. I could tell he hadn't been in Vietnam long. He didn't know the military jargon. I wondered if he had been to basic training. *I smell a rat,* I thought.

"Al, if I had known about that law, maybe I would have tried it too, but I'm such a heathen I don't think anybody would believe I wanted to become a preacher. I really admire you for wanting to serve the Lord. You seem the kind of man who is deeply concerned about the state of people's souls. My hat's off to you." *You lying sack of shit.*

Al did not acknowledge my complement. He may have realized I had seen through his scheme. The group was silent. We watched a few soldiers body surfing. It was Al who brought up the subject of politics, which in 1970 meant mostly Vietnam. The discussion started quietly, but soon became just Al ranting against the war.

Most young people lean left in political opinion, and I was no exception then. Few supported the war any longer. I agreed with most of what he said until he attacked the rich and privileged. From my position, he exemplified wealth and privileged and his left leaning politics couldn't change that.

"Whoa, whoa, wait a minute, Al. You'd better find another way to relieve your guilt. Look in the mirror. You are the poster child for wealth and privilege. You're a senator's son. You went to fucking Harvard. Your daddy's probably richer than shit. You've got a body guard, Al. You've got a fucking body guard. Where's mine? You have a cushy job at *Stars and Stripes* which you more than likely got just because of who you are, and you have cooked up this scheme to go home without finishing your tour of duty. Al, you are exactly what you hate."

"Yeah, well, I'm going to be president," he said.

"BULL SHIT, AL. What mother doesn't tell her son do good in school and someday you might grow up to be president. What makes you think you are so special?"

The thought that he was not special unnerved him, as though he had never considered it. He stood, then said to his entourage, "Let's go." They stood and followed him away, and as they did the lyrics of a popular Creedence Clearwater Revival anti-draft song came to mind:

> *It ain't me. It ain't me. I ain't no senator's son.*
> *It ain't me. It ain't me. I ain't no fortunate one.*

I wondered if the songwriter knew Al. Before he was out of earshot I called to him, "Hey, Al, I wouldn't vote for you to be dog catcher."

I had no idea that his father had groomed him all his life for the presidency, and I had no idea how close he would come to achieving his goal.

35

I set my chin on the chin rest of a Biomicroscope at the hospital in Chu Lai. "Oh, my, that's quite a lesion you've got there," Major Steiner, the ophthalmologist, said.

"A doctor in Duc Pho said there was nothing wrong with my eye. He was sending me back to the field, but another doctor happened to come by. He said the same as you."

"Do you remember the first doctor's name?" I told him and he wrote it on a prescription pad, but he did not say what he planned to do with it.

"Without proper care, you will lose this eye."

"Oh, shit, you're kidding. Am I?"

"No, we can save it. I'm sending you back to the States."

"Great! I don't have much time left here, but every little bit helps."

"Where do you live?"

"Atlanta." He looked at a list.

"Looks like Martin Army Hospital at Fort Benning in Columbus, Georgia is as close as I can get you to home. How far is it from Atlanta to Columbus?"

"Eighty miles, but that's a hell of a lot closer than I am now. Thanks."

"See me in the morning. I'll have your orders ready. You will go from here to Da Nang and from Da Nang to the States. In the meantime, put this in your eye every four hours." Two days later, I lay in the transient hospital at Da Nang. It was air-conditioned.

I was an ambulatory patient, which meant I could walk unassisted. I had never heard the term. We rode in a school bus headed to a C141medevac aircraft.

The ambulatory patients were first to board the airplane, then those in wheelchairs. A bus with special racks brought those on litters, and with them the mood changed to one of quiet reverence, and I counted my blessings. Seeing so many in such agony cut deep in me. My eye problem was nothing compared to what these men suffered. Some would not survive the journey.

Sounds did not carry far in the plane. The lighting was gentle and almost blue. Litter patients lined the walls, stacked in racks three high. Those who were able sat in the center facing the rear. Six or eight nurses worked together in precision like the changing of the guard at Buckingham Palace. I have been in churches that felt less holy than the interior of this aircraft.

To my right sat an older man, *too old for the military*, I thought, then I recognized him.

"Command Sergeant Major Hern, I'm Rinehart. We met when you came out to the field a few weeks ago."

"Oh, yes, Rinehart, I remember you. Did you get wounded?"

"No." I told him about my eye.

"Why are you here, Sergeant Major?"

"My heart, I had a slight heart attack just a few days after I met you. You know I was retiring. I guess I stayed a day or two longer than I should have."

A few weeks before my assignment to the mortar platoon at San Juan Hill, a helicopter landed while we were out on patrol. Command Sergeant

Major Hern stepped off it. Captain Yeager greeted him, then the Sergeant Major spoke to our company.

"Men, I've been in this man's army since 1942. I fought my way across Europe in World War II and fought in Korea. I've done two tours here in Vietnam, mostly behind a desk. Now, I am about to retire, but before I do, I want to spend one more night in the field with you troops. I hope you don't mind. I love you guys, and I love the Army."

"We don't mind, Sergeant Major. We are glad you are here," someone called out.

"I'm proud to serve with a man who fought in World War II," I added, and I was.

That evening I talked with Sergeant Major Hern until dark. From him, I learned much about soldiering. On our long flight, he told me about his life.

"I grew up on a scrabble dirt farm in East Tennessee during the Great Depression," he said. "President Roosevelt, God bless him, still had not brought an end to the Depression when the war started. I grew up poor, but hell, I didn't know it.

"In 1940, Hitler was running all over Europe and Japan, the East. Still many Americans wanted to stay out of the fight, but when Japan attacked Pearl Harbor, that was it. I joined the Army."

"It was up to us to rid the world of these evil empires. We did it. We brought home the bacon. America loved us for it. The civilian population treated us like conquering heroes.

A nurse brought a glass of water and Sergeant Hern's medication, a red pill and two white ones. He swallowed them then drank the water. Another nurse put eye drops in my eye, then we returned to our conversation.

"The first time I killed a man, I jumped into a shell crater and a German soldier was already in it. My rifle was in my hand. His wasn't. I fired and he died, then I lay with his corpse for four or five hours and in his blood. I got to know him pretty well. He was a human. He had a face and I still see it. His blood stained my clothes. For days, he was still with me, reminding me of what I had done."

Our conversation stop again while the nurses served the first of three meals. Sergeant Major Hern ate slowly without talking much, then fell asleep. I wished I could do the same but it didn't happen. I sat bored, awaiting his return to consciousness and when he did, he returned to our conversation as though he had never been absent.

"America remembers World War II as the good war," he said. It wasn't so good to the men who fought it, but it had to be done. Once you have felt war's pain, those who have not are like naive children to you.

"During my first tour in Vietnam, America still supported the war, but after years of seeing its realities on TV, they have had enough. In World War II, only the soldiers and sailors knew war's horrors. The civilians believed in the glory of it. The reasons for fighting were clear. It really was good against evil. People understood it.

"In Vietnam, the reasons for fighting are abstract. Nobody in America but the far left likes communism; even so, most Americans see no threat from North Vietnam, no compelling reason to fight so hard halfway around the world. Vietnam has become a bad war in the public's mind. The antiwar movement has branded you as bad soldiers."

"Were we good soldiers, Sergeant Major?"

"You did your duty. If you put the guys that fought along with me in World War II under your circumstances, they would do as you did, and if you were under theirs, you would do as they did. It's not the men who are different. It's the circumstances."

"Sergeant Major, I just want to forget about this and get on with my life. That's all. . ."

36

Three days later, after a short stay at Walter Reed Army Medical Center in Washington, my plane landed at Fort Benning, Georgia. It was early summer, not too hot yet, and the air and the sounds in the air all said, "You are in Georgia," and my eyes were satisfied as they looked upon the proper flora and fauna, and the sun hung just right in the sky. Good God, I was home. I had survived. By God I had survived intact, well, almost. I relaxed and when I did, only one thought filled me, Marianne. I had to make things right.

At Martin Army Hospital the next morning in a semi-private room, my roommate played a Creedence Clearwarter album on his eight-track tape player nonstop, all day, every day, and I did not mind. My rain had stopped.

"Good, you're awake. How do you feel?"

I looked up to see an angel or was it a nurse.

"Fine, my eye doesn't hurt. The epidural of the eye can't feel pain. Did you know that? I never gave it a minute's thought until this happened."

"Yes, I knew that. I'm a nurse, remember. Are you hungry?"

"Yes."

"You can go to the cafeteria and grab a bite. Dr. Hilton will see you in his office this afternoon at 2:00. The phone is on the nightstand if you want to call your wife or parents." She pointed to it on the nightstand.

"There is no wife, not even a girlfriend. I'm free as a bird," I said. *Free as a bird just like I wanted it, just . . . like . . . I . . . wanted it. Oh, God I gotta make it right.*

When I awoke from an afternoon nap, my mother stood above me crying. My dad stood next to her, my sixteen-year-old brother Doug looked over their shoulders.

"Well, there he is," Mom said as she wiped tears from her eyes.

"Hello, son," Dad said.

"Hey, Ricky," my brother said.

I hugged Mom, shook Dad's hand, and waved at Doug. "How is your eye?" Mom asked.

"They're going to operate on it tomorrow. I will be in an eye patch for a few weeks. After I lay around here for about a week, they say I can come home for a few days. I will lose some vision. They can't tell how much but I won't be twenty-twenty any longer."

"How are you, son?" Dad asked. By the way he said you, I knew he was asking about my state of mind, and I felt a new bond with my father, the bond of war, and I knew he wanted me to say, "I'm fine." For the first time, I wiggled and squirmed to fit myself into my pre-Vietnam mind. "I am just like I was when I left." I wanted it to be true, but I knew it wasn't. *He's been through this. He knows I am lying.*

After the operation, they gave me a sedative to make me rest for two days. My roommate said I kicked, tossed, and talked in my sleep. "You must have been having war dreams," but it wasn't so. I knew that in my dreams, I searched for Marianne. When I was able, I called her parents' home. Her mother answered the phone.

"Mrs. Morgan, this is Rick Rinehart. Marianne isn't by chance there, is she?"

"Oh, my goodness, Rick, there is nothing wrong. Is there? We heard you were in Vietnam. Are you home? Are you okay?"

"I'm okay but I'm in the hospital at Fort Benning. I wasn't wounded but there is a problem with my eye. I'll be good as new soon, just like before."

"I know your mother was worried sick. Come by sometime and see us. Marianne's dad always liked you. How much longer will you be in the Army?"

"Six months, unless they let me out early, and they are letting most Vietnam vets out early. They don't need us any longer. We just get in the way."

"Well, good."

"Mrs. Morgan, where is Marianne?"

"She has an apartment in Atlanta with two other girls. Why?"

"I need to talk with her. May I have her number?"

"Rick, you are a good boy, but no. She is marrying in a few weeks and I don't think it appropriate."

Boy? What the fuck have I got to do to be a man?

"Oh . . . I see . . . Thank you, goodbye."

I hung up. *Bitch.*

Married? . . . To whom? That Georgia Tech guy she was with at Travis's wedding? He's in the Air Force, a pilot. Marianne's mom would love that! I'm going to call Travis and find out.

"Hello," Travis answered.

"Travis."

"Rick! God almighty damn boy, it's good to hear your voice. You okay?"

We talked for a half hour before I asked about Marianne.

"I hear Marianne is getting married, is that true?"

"Yeah."

"To who? That guy she was with at your wedding?"

"Yeah, Nancy is a bride's maid."

"Have you got her phone number? I need to talk with her."

"Nancy has it. I'll put her on the phone."

Nancy and I talked for a quarter-hour, repeating much of what I had told Travis before I asked for Marianne's number.

"Will you give me Marianne's phone number? I need to speak with her."

"Don't call her, Rick. It's too late. She was devastated when you quit calling. It took her a year to get over it. She's happy now. Leave her alone."

"I gotta talk to her. I am back now. My war is over. I can be me again."

"Rick, I've known you all my life. I love you like a brother, but I am not going to be the one that gives you Marianne's number. Don't mess this up for her. Leave her alone."

"Okay, okay, okay."

Damn it, I'll get it from Jake. I need to call him anyway.

We talked for a few more minutes and ended the conversation on a happy note.

I called Jake. "Hey, man, you back?" he said.

"Yeah."

"Good, you okay?"

I told him about my eye. "What have you been up to?"

"Oh, taking a few graduate classes. I work at the Bay Station where we used to buy our beer."

"What about your draft status?"

"It's tied up in court, could take years. Hopefully, the draft will be over before there is a decision. Congress is talking about doing away with it. Did you hear about that?"

"Yeah, I heard. Listen, do you have Marianne's phone number? I need to talk to her."

"Yeah, Alice knows it." He called to her, "Hey, Alice, what's Marianne's phone number?"

His voice returned to me. "404 555 1962." I wrote it down.

"Where does she live?"

Jake called to Alice again.

"Riverbend Apartments H218," I heard Alice without Jake having to repeat it.

"She is getting married. Did you know?" Jake said.

"I heard."

"I don't guess I'll see you at the wedding?"

"Of course not."

"Well, come see us when you can."

"I will as soon as I get a little leave. I'll call you when I do. Talk to you later." We hung up, and I called Marianne.

"Hello," she said.

"Marianne," I said. She didn't say anything.

"Marianne." She sighed.

"Marianne. . . Marianne."

"Nancy said you might call."

"Marianne."

"Why did you wait so long? It's too late. It's over. It's long over." She hung up.

I tried to call again but no one answered. The next day when I called, her roommate said she was not there. I tried several more time, each filled with hope, but her roommate always intervened with,

"She isn't here." *I'll go see her, in three more days, I have leave.*

I grabbed a cab to the bus station. Dad picked me up at Greyhound in Atlanta. Mom had prepared a family meal for me as if it were Thanksgiving.

I ate, trying to hide my impatience, but failed. "Slow down, Ricky. You are eating so fast," Mom said. I slowed through the rest of the meal.

"That eye patch is cool," my youngest brother, eight-year-old Brian, said.

"It's way cooler to see with two eyes."

"Well, who wants a slice of pecan pie?"

"I'll have some later. I'm stuffed, can't eat another bite. I'm going out to see some friends and shake some of this food down." I stood and stretched.

"Oh, Ricky, I thought we would spend the evening together as a family."

"Mom, I'll be here three days. We'll have plenty of time together."

I got in my Volkswagen, turned the key, but nothing happened. *Shit, the battery is dead.* After pounding my hands on the steering wheel, I went inside and humbly asked to use the family car. They agreed.

Riverbend Apartments was a forty-minute drive from my parent's house. On the way, I noticed that I still wore my uniform. I meant to change.

I found her apartment and knocked on the door. *This is it. This is it.* But a stranger peeked through the partly opened door. *Her roommate, I guess.*

"Is Marianne here?"

"You must be that creepy ex-boyfriend that keeps calling her. No, she's not here. She is shopping for her wed . . .ing . . .dress. She is getting married. Get it!" The door slammed in my face.

She didn't know it, but she told me exactly where to find Marianne. I knew she would buy her dress at Rich's in Lenox Square Mall. We had looked at them there once together, though we had made no plans for a wedding yet. On the way, traffic snarled. *Move, move, move, go on, good God, get out of my way.* I beat on the steering wheel again. I had to get there before she left.

The traffic was no better in the parking lot. *I don't think anybody in Atlanta is at home. They are all in their cars.* I found a parking place in the far end of the lot and ran to the mall. Inside, I pushed my way through the crowded corridor, running as if I had stolen something and the law was hot on my trail.

I found Marianne in a wedding dress, admiring it in a large mirror. The sight of her slammed against me, as if I had bounced off an invisible barrier. I stepped back. I had never seen a more perfect bride. Then I remember she was not wearing it for me.

"Marianne," I said.

"Rick, what are you doing here? Oh, what happened to your eye? Are you back? You okay? You're still in your uniform. You still in the Army?" I saw confusion in her eyes and I saw delight, and I knew she still cared.

"Don't do it, Marianne, don't do it." Her fiancée stepped forward. He wore the uniform of a First Lieutenant in the Air Force.

"Rick, this is my fiancé, Blake." I paid no attention to him.

"Don't do it, Marianne."

"Specialist, you are out of line." He addressed me by Army rank. I still paid no attention to him.

"Marianne."

"Specialist."

"Don't do it."

Lieutenant Blake Hamlin was a small man, a highly skilled fighter pilot. I was in the best shape of my life and trained to kill. I was surprised when he blindsided me on the side of my face with all the strength he had. It barely fazed me. I could have destroyed him then and there, but I did the smartest thing of my life. I took a dive. I hit the floor, and Marianne leaned over me in the wedding dress.

"Rick, are you okay?" She scowled at her fiancée.

"Yeah, yeah, I'm okay."

"Leave him alone," she said to Blake.

"I suggest you leave, Specialist," Blake said.

"Better go," Marianne said.

"Okay, okay." I walked away but I felt Marianne's eyes. I knew she still cared. I knew she was making a mistake, and I knew if I had fought with Blake, she would never forgive me. Marianne always sides with the underdog, but no matter. The wedding still happened.

A few weeks later, I drove my Volkswagen to Brooks, Georgia and parked my car out of sight near the First Methodist Church, and from behind a large crepe myrtle with purple blooms I watched as she and Blake walked out of the church into a shower of rice. God had never created a more beautiful bride.

I cried at the sight of her.

37

I did not know whether America would survive.
Reading the history today doesn't capture the fear,
the fear that swept America in the late sixties and
early seventies. War protests and rioting blacks,
Americans were in the news again and again. The
riots were only news stories until I returned to
Columbus from Atlanta on the bus one night. The
Greyhound station sat on Broad Street, and Broad
Street was on fire.

     I saw black men running and police cars and
fire trucks traveling the streets, some slowly
cruising, and some racing by. Police and fire sirens
filled the space between the buildings. Red and blue
emergency lights used the same space, alternating

their colors in my eyes. The flashing lights and the glow from the fire and the sounds hid the real. I had stepped off into an abstraction of Columbus, Georgia. Was this really happening?

As I got off, I asked the driver what was going on. "Beats me, I just got here, too. Looks like a riot. Glad I'm spending the night in Dothan." He drove the bus away.

I went into the terminal. The ticket clerk and I were the only people there. I did not notice where the others from the bus went.

"What's going on?" I asked.

"The cops were trying to arrest this black guy for armed robbery. The police got in a shoot-out with him. He got killed and now everybody's pissed off. Hosea Williams is here." Hosea Williams was a Civil Rights activist from Atlanta.

"Is there a taxi here? I got to get to Fort Benning."

"No. There is a curfew. Nobody is supposed to be on the streets. I hoped nobody would get off that bus, especially a white man. I'm closing up and getting the hell out of here."

"You gonna lockup? Shit, I'll get killed out there. You can't leave me standing here."

"Let me see what I can do." He called a cab company. In less than five minutes, a cab screeched up to the back door.

"Get in," the driver called out. I did. "Let's get the fuck out of here," he said. We screeched away and headed to Fort Benning.

A few days later, I watched the evening news with a group of friends in the chow hall at the hospital. On the news, a young man dressed in pieces from a military uniform as though he had come straight from the front lines of an imaginary war testified before a Congressional committee in his New England upper-class accent that seemed contrived to me. What he said sounded even more contrived.

His half-truths and lies became fact in America's mind, adding to the myth that Vietnam vets were monsters. The demonization of vets was a tactic used by the anti-war activist. So effective were these attacks that Vietnam vets felt their repercussion all their lives. In past wars, being a veteran was an asset in the job market, to the Vietnam vet, it was a liability. The young man told the committee:

They told the stories at times they had personally raped, cut off ears, cut off heads, taped wires from portable telephones to human genitals and turned up the power, cut off limbs, blown up bodies, randomly shot at civilians, razed villages in fashion reminiscent of Genghis Khan, shot cattle and dogs for fun, poisoned food stocks, and generally ravaged the countryside of South Vietnam in addition to the normal ravage of war, and the normal and very particular ravaging which is done by the applied bombing power of this country. . . . The country doesn't know it yet, but it has created a monster, a monster in the form of millions of men who have been taught to deal and to trade in violence, and who are given the chance to die for the biggest nothing in history; men who have returned with a sense of anger and a sense of betrayal which no one has yet grasped.

All at my table were Vietnam vets, several of them were badly wounded there. Someone said, "What unit was that guy in? They must have been some badasses."

"He's not talking about his unit. He's talking about us all," another man said.

"Why would he want to talk about us like that?"

"He wants the war to end."

"So do I. We are handing it over to the Vietnamese. It's ending."

"Maybe he really wants us to hand it over to the Viet Cong," another guy said. Everyone laughed . . . but just a little.

"How many heads do you have?" someone asked.

"Four, all children."

"I didn't see anybody do anything like that, except, 'Raze villages in a fashion reminiscent of Genghis Khan'," one of the guys said mocking his snooty accent, especially the way he said the word Genghis.

"I think I will go tape some telephone wires to someone's balls. That's always good for giggles," another man said as he walked away, laughing out loud.

"Who is that stupid son of a bitch, anyway?"

"Fuck, I don't know. Jane Fonda's buddy, I think."

"His name is John Kerry," I said. We had no idea that he would be the Senator from Massachusetts, a presidential candidate, and Secretary of State.

"He's an idiot. Fuck him," someone said.

The country has created a monster John Kerry told Congress. I guess I'm one of those monsters. . .

The Army assigned me to a convalescent job at the hospital until I recovered. Then they sent me to Fort Carson, Colorado where I was a clerk until my discharge. Just like that, my military service was over. "Do not pass go. Do not collect two-hundred dollars." Go home now. Get out of here. Go get a job and live the American dream. Bye Bye. I went back to Atlanta.

Not long after the army discharged me, I went to see Jake in Carrollton. I had not seen the campus since my graduation fiasco a year and a half ago. Before going to his place, I drove through campus. They were building some new dorms. Other than that, it looked the same.

Jake looked the same also, but his hair had grown longer and his dress hipper. He wore bell bottom jeans, a flowered shirt, and boots with high heels. The boots made him seem taller and slimmer than he was. Alice wore an ankle length flowered skirt and blouse with no bra. I noticed she let the

hair under her arms grow. Some found that sexy. I
didn't.

They lived in a single-wide trailer in a trailer
park on Lovern Road, about two miles from the
school. The trailer was not nice, but it was adequate.
They had little furniture and what they had looked
worn. Jake had covered the walls in rock and roll
posters. We greeted and hugged, then Jake sat in a
well-worn La-Z-boy chair, which was his place.
Alice and I sat on the sofa. Jake turned off the TV
and played the same Doors album Carter played
back in Vietnam. "Come on baby light my fire,"
filled the room.

"I can offer you a joint or a beer," Jake said.

"I'll take the beer. I'm looking for a job and
some places test for drugs."

"Yeah, I hear that. Fortunately, the Bay
Station is not that smart," he said as he rolled a joint.
"I go to work stoned all the time." Alice brought a
beer to me then joined Jake in his smoke.

"We're having free-range chicken tonight. We
eat healthy now, don't want any extra chemicals in
our bodies." He said as he passed the joint back to
Alice.

"Do you have any idea how many hormones
they feed regular chickens these days?" Alice said.

"No," I said. "What does free-range mean?"

"It means they were raised the old-fashioned way and not in a big chicken houses where they pack them in so close they can't move. They cut their beaks. It's horrible," Alice said.

"Yeah, horrible, I can't imagine," I said.

"Tomorrow is homecoming at the college. The guys at Foster's Store are turning Proud Mary into a float. You want to go?"

"Sure." I said. Jake called his 1953 Plymouth the Proud Mary. He took the name from a popular song.

"Proud Mary still run?" I asked.

"Barely, Alice and I drive a Toyota."

"I saw it outside. Nice car."

"You remember when they started importing them, we didn't know whether to call them Toy-otas or To-yotas," Jake said.

"Yeah, I remember that. Now they're everywhere. Who would have thought?"

"They got fraternities at the college now. They're all local, but it's a start. The guys at Fosters are kinda like a fraternity. Don't you think?"

"Foster's Store isn't much like a fraternity house though. Are they going to apply for a charter somewhere?" I said.

"No, some joined the Cavaliers. It's a local frat."

"Who lives at Foster's now?"

"Oh, you know them all," he said, then listed them. I remembered the names but could not put the names with a face.

Next morning, we went to Foster's Store. The guys had painted the Proud Mary pink with regular house paint and in grey they had painted peace signs and stop the war on the doors. I remembered the guys but didn't really know them. All were in costume, Native American headdress, striped prison shirts, and such. Jake wore an old top hat from my dad's store that I gave him years ago.

I took a bed sheet and made myself an Arab, but I was a grown man. College is an extended childhood and mine had ended with my draft notice. I knew things. I knew things these college boys will never know, and with God's blessing, they will never have to know.

People cheered our antiwar message as we rode by. To the unaffected, the antiwar movement was as much a fad as it was a conviction. Saying you are against the war was easy and hip. Peace signs were everywhere, even a fashion accessory. I smiled. I cut up with them, but I faked it. The war was not abstract to me.

38

I was born on the baby boomers' leading edge. We flooded the schools. We flooded the colleges. So much idealistic youth ripening in America simultaneously changed the culture, mostly for the better; even though we made all the mistakes common to the young. Now we were adults. We needed jobs.

Someone one year older than me faced a different world from mine. College graduates born in 1945 or before were scooped up by businesses as quickly as they graduated. When I got out of the army, the business world was flooded with baby boomer college graduates.

Time magazine's cover showed a young man in a cap and gown pumping gas. In those days, self-service gas stations did not exist, and gas station attendant was a low-paying job.

But I did well. It took four and a half months to get a job at Dun and Bradstreet as a financial analyst. It didn't pay much. The business world is a supply and demand place and it was filled with recent graduates. Legend has it that Moses dropped the eleventh commandment on his way down from the mountain. No doubt it was the law of supply and demand.

A friend and I leased an apartment in a singles apartment complex, planning to live the *Playboy* lifestyle, and I did. I had unsatisfying sex with beautiful women. I drank too much. I was cool, but I was empty. *Is this all there is?* I found no satisfaction in living only for myself. The *Playboy* philosophy was not working because it is not natural to not love, but who was I to love?

My search led me to the Second Sun, a singles bar on Peachtree. Drinks were inexpensive there. The bar was crowded with singles who mostly didn't know what was wrong in their lives any more than I did. I drank vodka and tonic with a twist of lime in those days -- or should I say nights, after night, after night.

Eric Clapton's song Layla was the favorite there. They played it over and over . . . night after night, after night.

Layla, you've got me on my knees
.

Eric Clapton and Duane Allman played guitar solos that sounded as if someone was crying, and inside I cried along with them. It was the only song I wanted to hear.

Later, I learned the story behind the song. Eric Clapton was in love with his friend's wife. He wrote it for her. His friend was Beatle George Harrison. Unlike Clapton, I pushed my love of Marianne into the cracks deep in my mind. I could not allow myself to think of her. Then one day I saw her at the car wash.

With the new job, came my new car. My sixteen-year-old brother drove my Volkswagen to death while I was in Vietnam. It barely ran. I bought a Coppertone 1970 Camaro 350. Rain and grime from the interstate had hidden its new shine within a few days. When the weather cleared, I took it to the car wash.

The Datsun Motor Company had not changed its name to Nissan yet. The long-nosed fastback Datsun 240Z was their entry into the sports car market. Its sporty design and low price made it a big success. I wanted to buy one, but there was a waiting list. I needed reliable transportation right away, so I bought the Camaro.

The car wash I used was the long tunnel type that automatically pulls your car through while you wait. I noticed a blue Datsun 240z as it went through in front of mine. As I walked down the hall, I admired it through the windows that overlooked the car wash. It was what I wanted, down to the color. I walked into the waiting room and Marianne stood there looking through a window at her car as it came through. She was pregnant.

"Oh." Every emotion from love of her to hatred of Blake ran through my body in such rapid succession that I heard a buzzing sound my head. "Oh," I said again, "It's you."

"Hello, Rick," she said in a low, soft voice. The squirting water's sound and the roaring electric engines filled the silence. She watched her car and did not look directly at me, but I was unable to keep my eyes off her. *She's pregnant. She's pregnant. Damn it. It should be mine.*

"You're pregnant."

"Only a month left." Now she stood at the window, standing so close to the glass that her breath fogged it.

"I love your car."

"Me, too, I'm not surprised you like it." She still looked through the window.

"Yes, it is what I would have bought, but I didn't have the time to wait for one, so I bought the Camaro."

"It's nice, too," she said. The workers finished drying her car. "It was good seeing you again, Rick," she said as she opened the door to go out. She walked to her car with short fast steps as if she feared looking back, and I prayed that she would. She drove away.

I stood feeling empty. I wanted her to stay, but because I couldn't have her always, I was glad to see her go. I couldn't see her face as she walked away, but I thought she was crying. As I drove, my hands shook and I could not concentrate. At the Second Sun, I ordered a vodka tonic with a twist of lime and then another . . . and . . . then . . . another. . . .

Layla, I'm begging darling please.

39

When I was eighteen, my friend, Dave, noticed that the little dots in the print on the comic strip character, the Phantom, were the same as the little dots in the date of birth box on a draft-card. The draft card's dots were there to keep people from changing the birth date by erasing it. He cut the dots from the Phantom's pants, carefully taped it over the date box on his draft-card with Scotch tape, copied both sides with a copy machine, changed the date, then laminated front to back with a laminating machine and *voila* a fake ID. He made one for me, and with our fake ID, Dave and I went into my first bar, a folk music club called the Bottom of the Barrel.

I had not been there, nor had I seen Dave in several years, but on this night, I had a date with a folksy type girl who I thought would enjoy it. Dave, and his new wife, Martha, happened to be there. Dave was working on his doctorate in history at Georgia State. We renewed our friendship. He had grown a beard. He introduced me to Martha. They looked in love. He held her hand, looking at her with newlywed eyes. Martha wore her dark hair long, hanging to the middle of her back. She was tall. Both dressed like hippies. Martha taught at a Montessori School in northeast Atlanta.

They lived in Atlanta's Virginia Highland section often called just the Highlands. Today it is a trendy, neighborhood filled with chic restaurants, coffeehouses, and bars, but in 1972, the neighborhood was declining. Their house was built in the 1920's in the craftsman style with a front porch, hardwood floors, a fireplace in the living room, and high ceilings.

Not far from the corner of Virginia and Highland Avenues sat a working man's bar called Moe's and Joe's. It opened in 1947 and looks the same today as it did then, long and narrow with a bar on one side, booths on the other, and walls of pine paneling. The food was good and the beer was cold, which is the most important thing for a working man's bar.

Dave and I often drank there while discussing the world's problems, history, and even philosophy. His friendship was a welcome break from the cold calculation of the polyester business suit singles scene in which I lived. I took refuge from my soulless world with Dave and Martha in their softer blue jean world of the Highlands. I liked it better there.

My job was dull dribble, but most jobs are dull dribble. I didn't complain, but sometimes an emptiness of everything I was doing filled me and I asked the classic question. *Is this it? Is this all there is?*

Going from an adrenaline filled war to a desk job is like caging a lion. That's why they call it work, not play. That's why they pay you to do it, and I knew that. I pushed my feelings aside. Some days I left the office to call on businesses in person. Those were the best days at my job.

Barton International Recruiters of Atlanta matched prospective employees and overseas jobs. A Vietnam vet friend found a job through them guarding oil wells in Saudi Arabia. "All I do is ride around in a Jeep and they pay me seventy-thousand dollars a year to do it," he told me. Seventy-thousand dollars a year was three times a typical salary then. My boss sent me to write a financial report on Barton.

I looked at my note for the address. Barton International, 127 Peachtree, The Candler Building, Suite 525 it said.

Coca-Cola magnate Asa Candler built the Candler building in 1904. At seventeen stories, it stood taller than any other building in Atlanta then.

Modern skyscrapers grew in Atlanta like wild weeds. None had the Candler building's dignity. In the lobby, the stairway's handrail and newel post contained a marble sculpture of lions. The walls were marble, and the floor carpeted. Doors and handrail were made of polished brass, and a large brass and crystal chandelier hung in the lobby. The building was grand, time-hardened like a wise grandfather as it oversaw its glass and steel children growing in the city around it.

I found Suite 525, walked in. A secretary stopped typing and greeted me with the standard, "May I help you?" I explained the reason for my call. She led me to her boss.

Dan Barton sat at his desk with his feet propped on it. He wore cowboy boots and a suit, too western in style for Atlanta's tastes, but it told me he did things his way. I liked him immediately. We chatted, then I asked some financial question.

"Hell," he said, "I'm the only asset this company has. It all depends on me recruiting men like you to get rich in Saudi Arabia, and it ain't too hard to convince men to get rich. All it takes is me, a desk, a telephone, and that sweet little secretary out there. There are no real assets other than me. It's about quitting time. Come on, let's go get a beer. You can write your bull crap later."

"Well, okay," I said. We walked to the Cock and Bull, bellied up to the bar, and ordered beers. Dan took a big swig, wiped his lips with the back of his hand and said, "How long have you been back from Nam?"

"How did you know I served in Vietnam?"

"You've gotten it written all over you. I was one of the first troops there and I stayed until the end of Tet in sixty-eight. I was a Green Beret, and I know what you are going through because I've been through it. You hate this Mickey Mouse job, don't you?"

"Hell, yeah," I said. I had never allowed myself to admit I hated my job.

"Why don't you quit the Mickey Mouse Club and go to work with some real men in Saudi?" Over the next hour and two more beers, he explained the job to me. He planted the bait but I didn't bite. He gave me his card. "Call me if you change your mind." I put the card in my wallet and went to the Second Sun and continued to drink to midnight. I switched to my usual vodka and tonic.

Dave's wife, Martha, was a gourmet cook. She invited me to a dinner party. The guests were mostly graduate students, Dave's friends from Emory and Georgia State. I knew some of them and some I did not.

Dr. Balbo, Dave's doctorate adviser, was there. Dave had introduced me to him at Moe's and Joe's. He was of the World War II generation, tubby, jolly, and dressed in a tweed jacket, and he smoked a pipe, as you might expect a professor would do. If his hair and beard were white, he would have made an excellent Santa Claus.

He told a story about his military experience. "I joined the army in nineteen-thirty-six. They assigned me to a Calvary unit, and by Calvary I don't mean modern internal combustion engine Calvary. I mean Calvary with horses and swords.

"I am damn glad the United States Army in its infinite wisdom changed its mind about horse Calvary before the war started, or I wouldn't be sitting here tellin' stories."

Everyone laughed.

"How long were you in the Army?" One of the guests asked.

"To the end of the war. Were you in the military?" Dr. Balbo asked the man.

"I served for twenty-years as a B-52 pilot. I'm retired now."

"Were you in Vietnam?" I asked.

"We flew missions there all the time. I was stationed in Okinawa."

"I was a lowly infantry man in there," I said.

A friend of Dave's sat on the sofa with his wife. I didn't know them. They said almost nothing to the other guest, but listened intently, and I got the feeling we were being judged. His dress was ten years behind the times and he wore his hair the same way. She was small, blond, fragile looking, and dressed too conservatively for a young woman. Her dress made me feel she was prudish. Both worked on advanced psychology degrees of some sort at Emory.

The woman nudged her husband. He did not look at her. They stood together. He took her hand. With the woman leading, they walked to the door as Martha walked from the kitchen wearing an apron and carrying a bottle of wine. She stopped. "Are you leaving?"

"I'm not eating with baby killers," the woman said as they walked out. The door latch made a loud click which added finality to their departure.

I sat quietly.

Dr. Balbo was red with anger.

"Well, I suppose we had better go. I can see we are not wanted here," the B52 pilot said to his wife. Martha asked them to stay, but to no avail. The pilot helped his wife with her coat and the door clicked with the same finality as they left.

Next day, I called Dan Barton, "Is that job still available in Saudi Arabia."

"Yes."

"Fuck this country. I'll take it."

40

My parents took me to the airport. I left my car parked out of sight under a car cover in their backyard. We ate a parting meal at Spondivits, a seafood restaurant near the airport. It was a favorite haunt of singles and always crowded. Spondivits looked as if it sat in the gentle breeze on the beach of a Caribbean island, but it rumbled with the noise of Atlanta's airport.

On the way to the restroom, I noticed Marianne's husband, Blake, sitting in a booth near the bar area. The crowd blocked my view of Marianne, seated across from him.

I stood at the urinal, light-headed, trying to decide whether to speak or go back to my table another way. I put my hand on the wall for support, took a stabilizing breath, and walked to the table. From the direction I came, I would be facing Marianne. Only . . . it wasn't Marianne. Blake looked into a blond flight attendant's eyes with love . . . or was it lust. I spoke as I went by.

"Hello, Blake." He looked confused as if he was trying to place me, and I don't think he did. Our encounter at Rich's was brief, and when we last met, I wore a patch over my eye.

"Hello," he said as I walked away.

I took a cruel satisfaction in what I had seen, at the same time I hurt for Marianne. The satisfaction came because I knew I would have been a better husband to Marianne than him. The hurt came because I knew he was not good to her. Marianne would not live a life in love, her husband a fraud, his love a fraud. But I had caused her ruin. She did not leave me. Blake did not interfere in our love. She didn't know him then. I pushed her away. I caused this. I destroyed her happiness and mine. All I could do now was to make the best of it and push on.

I cannot say I liked Saudi Arabia. It is not a happy place. I don't think even the Saudis like it. But I liked my job and the men with whom I worked at Brown and Root. We built oilfield infrastructure, refineries, and such. They paid me well and, most of the money was tax-free.

Brown and Root gave us a two-week vacation every three months to get away from the tedium of Saudi Arabia. I spent my time in Europe seeing the sights.

On a visit to London with Richard, a coworker, he introduced me to Julie, his wife's friend which started a romance fueled by the money I made, traveling Europe together and good sex. Starting in Amsterdam, we cruised the Rhine, Main, and Danube rivers visiting Cologne, Vienna, Bratislava, and Budapest. It was a high point in my life.

Everything Julie did was feminine. When she moved, her body pulled on my eyes. Her blond hair hung to her shoulders with a slight curl, making her look more like a Swede than an Englishwoman. We spent our afternoons on the deck, enjoying the sights as we leisurely drank wine and at night we rocked the boat, literally. We talked of marriage.

I had a decision to make. My contract with Brown and Root was ending. Did I want to be an international person, working job after job overseas and marry Julie? It would be a long-distance relationship. She would live in London, keeping her job at Bloomsbury, a publishing house. I would work anywhere I found employment in the Middle East in the oil industry. I had friends who lived this lifestyle. Julie had a decision to make as well. Could she live her life this way?

I did not sign a new contract, choosing instead to go home. International workers of my type often spent a few months or even years before returning. Once a person had experience in this kind of work, future employment comes easily. When I landed in Atlanta, I did not know if I would return to the Middle East, marry Julie, or stay in Atlanta.

Just before I left Saudi Arabia, I received a letter from Travis.

Dear Rick,

I know it's been a while since you heard from me. Hope you are well over there in wherever the hell you are. I can't imagine living that far from home. Everything is fine here. Nothing much has changed since my last letter, but I do have some news. Marianne has filed for a divorce. She called Nancy last night. It seems Blake had a problem keeping on his pants.

Marianne was a self-inflicted wound. Time had healed it. I had trained myself to not want her. I was happy, but home was sad. There was love, but there was baggage, all the karma left behind.

I found a furnished apartment in an older building in midtown Atlanta with a six-month lease. I was home. I had an apartment. I had money. Now what?

Nothing. . . Absolutely nothing, I did not call Travis. I did not call Jake. I slept a lot.

After six weeks of my self-imposed isolation, Travis called, "What in the hell are you doing? Why haven't you called me?"

"How did you know I came home?"

"I called your mother. Get your ass up here to Cartersville and visit me. Nancy's cooking dinner for you Saturday and you had better be here to eat it."

"Okay, okay."

Travis and Nancy lived in an old house, so old that it predated European settlement of north Georgia. It is a forgotten fact of history that many Cherokees lived like white plantation owners, only to be up rooted and marched all the way to Oklahoma on the Trail of Tears. Often, the current old home's owner does not know his house was built by a Cherokee.

Travis and Nancy were renovating one. The house was not as grand as some, a white two-story with redbrick chimneys at each end and a porch across the front. It sat in a green valley away from town, with blue mountains sculpting the horizon. *We've come a long way since Foster's store,* I thought as I pulled in to the drive.

I rang the doorbell.

"Well, the prodigal son has returned. Come in, come in, Nancy has run to the store for some last-minute things. How have you been? You look great, all tan and everything."

"I'm fine. I love your place."

"Yeah, well, it's plenty of work. I hope we haven't bitten off more than we can chew. We put in these hardwood floors. Our contractor will start remodeling the kitchen in about a month."

"Does the fireplace work?"

"Believe it or not, it does. A mason checked it out before we built our first fire in it."

I heard the kitchen door open and Nancy call out. "Rick, you here all ready?"

Before I could answer, a three year-old-girl ran into the living room with a toy packaged in a difficult to open plastic clamshell package.

"Uncle Travis, will you open this for me," she said.

"Is this your niece?"

Travis didn't answer. He looked beyond me.

"What?" I said. Travis smiled.

I turned. There stood Marianne. . .

41

We are old men now, Travis, Jake, and I. Young men look forward to the future. Old men live in the past. Young men are writing their stories as they go, and the old men are reading theirs as they reflect and drawing conclusions from what they have learned. Perhaps their conclusions are what life is about.

How many times have you heard old men say, "I tried to tell him, but he wouldn't listen." A truth heard is not as valid as a truth lived.

Foster's Store is still standing. No doubt the progress of man will bulldoze it for a strip mall or some such thing. I was to meet Jake and Travis there, but the city had widened the road over the parking lot and there is no break in the curb for it.

We parked at the nearby CVS Pharmacy. There, we leaned against our cars and talked as we had done when we were young. Then we walked to Foster's Store. We peeked through the window.

"I wonder if anyone has a key." Jake said.

"This is good enough," Travis said as he shaded his eyes from the sun to better see.

"It's not much to see anyway," I said.

"What time does the game start?' Travis asked.

"One o'clock," Jake answered.

The University of West Georgia had a football team now. It came years after our time. We had not been to a game.

"Good," I said, "That will give us time to catch up." Years had gone by since we had seen each other.

"How are Marianne and the kids?" Travis asked.

"Marianne is well and the kids are finally out of the house. Jana works for Ely Lilly. Jason took after his grandpa. He's a pilot, and Mandy is a senior here at West Georgia. We will see her at the game."

Marianne and I waited three months before marrying, after Travis brought us back together, and my life with her was as God intended a life should be.

Each of us is a story. Mine with Marianne was a happy one. Without man stories, God would have nothing to do but run the universe, and that is a dull business. We are God's fun . . . and we are his frustration.

Another books by Bob O'Kelley

Bad

Roads

for

Good Men

The Courageous
Contractors of the
Iraq War

BOB O'KELLEY

Titles written under the pen name Roland O'Conner

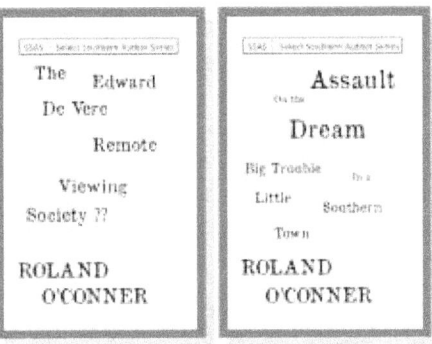

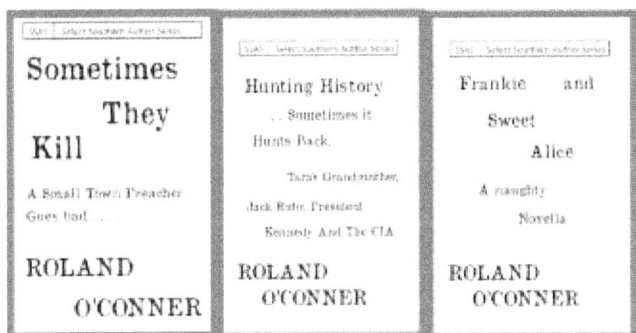